Paperback Comedian

A Novella Trilogy

E. C. Flickinger

A Hilltop Book

Grackle Publishing - Ambler, Pennsylvania

Hilltop

An imprint of Grackle Publishing, LLC

gracklepublishing.com

ISBN: 978-0-9982069-3-6 (hc.)
ISBN: 978-0-9982069-2-9 (pbk.)
ISBN: 978-1-951620-02-8 (ebook)

For Sarah and Jim

Lust

Anything is possible.

The hilltop in the distance is barely visible. Cast your dice and move that many squares forward.

Four. One, two, three, four. Water seeps through an outcrop. A bamboo pipe diverts a portion into an immense stone bowl carved from the face of the mountain.

Sam

THE birds were out before the rain. A long-billed plover stood guard at the cupped edge of a loosely tethered spout. The smoky brown pole swayed as the wind whispered an unfamiliar song.

"Pip pip pip!" cried the plover, launching a thousand bird-cousins who roused a legion of quivers. Wave after wave of needle-arrows cut through the heraldic blue sky. All went silent.

Madame? Monsieur? With a flap or two of anxious wings, M. Plover rose above the fray, circling the water before settling on the wall of the fountain. But what skirred the birds from the trees, off the bushes? What made the plover cry "Pyuoo!"?

There! *Causa ruckus*! Despite his likely mischief, he was not one of the usual suspects: not flatworm, nor souse, nor fountain yenta. He looked old, half spent. He sat sloppily in wrinkled clothes, sporting mismatched paisley socks, navy blue pants, and a misbuttoned plaid shirt. The plover glowered at the old man, the ancient boy, the intolerable danger. If it were not for honor, M. Plover would have raised the dragon banner and clawed his eyes out.

A fever began to stir in the forest. A wildfire of rumor spread from tree to tree. The plovers gathered under the majestic red pines in greater and greater numbers. Man or mouse, something had to be done.

Sam didn't wake that morning. He wasn't dead, though he certainly smelled the part. No, he was dreaming of something wonderful, something unbelievably sweet. He would have chosen this captivity over any freedom. He had no use for the real world.

Sam wasn't always such a lazy man. For years, he was a lazy boy. He spent his days and nights cloistered in his room, swirling in the same circles, spinning in tiny spaces only rain knew how to fill. Car horns and cries of children soothed him. In those moments, even with his eyes closed, he knew he wasn't alone.

Winter became spring became summer became fall. He kept all doors shut and was marked absent most of his life. Only Mom's homemade spaghetti had a fifty-fifty chance of rousting him from bed. When he did join the family, Sam liked to show off by slurping the last four inches of the long noodles.

Four, three, two, one. Dinner was over as the last noodle disappeared into Sam's cheek. He would have been a good squirrel—laughter filled the dining room.

"What?" Sam said with a straight face. He knew how to work a crowd.

Sam stacked plates on the kitchen counter. If it wasn't his turn for dishes, he'd head upstairs to tackle homework. Memorization seemed useless. All the dates and formulas were easily found if ever needed in real life. If someone wanted to know the number of degrees in a particular angle, couldn't they guess at it? Isn't an angle that looked about half way to forty-five degrees about twenty-two degrees? Oh no, what if an ice cream cone was at a sixty-degree angle, dripping like crazy, and the only way to save it was to know the exact angle between the cone and the falling drop?

Okay, okay, trying to shoot a rocket into space does deserve a decent formula. But who would ever need to remember Peter the Great? He was good and bad; he reformed this on this date and conquered that on that date. They don't really want you to know he drank too much and executed his eldest son for treason. Why would they? If schools taught morality, where would all the cosines go?

The nine o'clock siren signaled the end of day for all children save one. Sam might toss and turn for twenty minutes before sitting up in bed. He knew the world would soon be swallowed in silence. He needed to create some kind of racket to occupy his mind, to remind him why he clung to life.

Sam smiled at the trove of books on both sides of his bed: incoming on the left, finished on the right. The best books were bestowed a position of honor next to his pillow. The topmost book was his all-time favorite. He could reach out to tap its cover and be assured those characters were real. He often wondered what they were up to, where they were heading. He would lift the book off the stack to share the unbearable weight of their journey. With few exceptions, he hated reading any book twice as it would stall his finding the next masterpiece. But this book on the top of the pillow stack was turned cover to cover three times and still Sam dreamt of visiting those friends a fourth night.

He could hear raindrops dancing on the rooftop above. The faster the patter, the faster he read.

Peril hung precariously in air thick with tribulation. She had come too far to turn back. Her lithe body stretched, straightened, made ready to bear the weight of the final trial of her unmerciful quest. Her eyes circled the landscape. She instinctively reached for her sword....

These heroines were a drug to him, a fix for an incurable addiction. Not even all the king's men could put Sam back together as he reached her final page. He couldn't—he mustn't—ever look beyond the first paragraph of that page. He knew those words were meant to pull the threads from the cloth that bound them together. The pages where they met, where they lived, would break free and scatter. The merciless wind would spread her memory across the ages and she would fade from him.

He would resist each new word for as long as he could, if only to see the next sunrise, if only to hold her for one more day. The cold sting of losing her burned his soul yet he could not keep her from her fate any longer. He couldn't. He loved her too much. He needed to know she would be okay, that she could go on without him. For when her book closed, she would be gone—no matter how much he pleaded for another chapter.

Sam was nearly crying by the time he discovered how she had overcome all obstacles and could now see a familiar speck on the distant horizon. She was almost home. She was happy, more than happy: she was complete, now recast as her better self, a king—or queen if she so preferred. It was her choice how to rule all the lands as far as the eye could see.

Sam smiled as the mist turned to rain—it was the rain that made her touch her cheek, not a tear. The ambiguity soothed him. She remained strong for those who needed her strength. And even if she were crying—which she clearly wasn't—a king can cry. A king can write a law about how perfectly okay it is to cry when you're finishing a quest or when you can finally see your home on the horizon … or when you find the soul you'd love to marry.

Sam didn't feel much like reading after loneliness crept out from the shadows and joined the darkness for a cup of tea. Those two sat for hours without speaking a word until the sun rose and sent them on their way.

"Pyuoo!"

The plover's cry woke Sam but only for a moment. It would take nearly twenty minutes for the numbness to fade, for his fingers to interpret the sinewy weight balanced in his strong right hand. He clenched his fist once, maybe twice, then let go. A hollow rod bounced against curved stones before slapping the damp ground.

Why did this dream imagine him in such an uncomfortable position? Why did he feel so intoxicated?

Sam caught a glimpse of a reddish shape before a blinding light forced his eyes closed. When he tried to replay the falling object in his mind, images from his dream flashed before him: a laboratory, a large white table, faces he didn't recognize.

Sam kept his eyes shut. He was afraid to see this new world. Something had gone wrong; he was sure of it. This breathless blue feeling couldn't be normal.

The sound of water slowly filtered into his consciousness. He hadn't expected to hear the splatter differently in each ear. Was that a fountain gnawing at the back of his neck? Yes, he was out-of-doors, his duff in the dirt, his back against a cold stone wall. His shoulders were damp from errant splashes. What was he sitting in?

The sky turned bleak.

"Traitor!" Sam called out to the sun or sky or maybe one of those unknown faces who had abandoned him.

The wind's joy fell silent. Sam sat alone, far from home, in a puddle, on his birthday.

Addison

ADDISON too sat alone, hidden away in the tallest of towers, far beyond the reach of wonderment and cruelty. Her eyes burned for sleep. Her hands bled from hours of ripping and joining. She could not rest, even as yards upon yards of bloodstained fabric gathered at her feet.

She sensed a struggle in the distance. When she closed her eyes to think, her mind went fuzzy with doubt. Would she ever be free, free to don a warrior's armor, free to wander the dark forests of the distant west? How she ached to walk barefoot in the lush meadows outside these walls. A kitten circled her feet. She would miss Buttons—

A burst of thunder echoed mountain to mountain as a mysterious mist surrounded the castle. She found herself standing tall, arms raised for a fight. With palms facing outward, she slapped wildly at the suffocating fog. Her fury might have cast her as a young and troubled frog struggling to swim the moat, but she wasn't under any spell and she wasn't young, not anymore, having just turned sixteen. She would soon embark on a quest, a wondrous journey under a deep blue sky—no, under a perfect violet sky.

A tear startled her as it ran down her cheek—for she was brave and strong. Even at this most unusual height, where the air was far too thin, where the damp walls spiraled inward at an alarming pace, she would not be consumed by fear nor lulled into idleness. Yet, in these final breaths, when neither night nor day ruled the world, when all might perish in a single cast of dice, she lost her way. Her hands fell still. She now only dreamt of tying the last of her knots—

A high-pitched sound cried out, but she was too old to remember such childhood voices. The will-o'-wisps shouted in undecipherable whispers, begging her to run as her captors would soon return. She stirred to an odd feverish tapping on the arm of her chair. She took a deep breath and forced a smile. She did not fear the wind or rain, thunder or lightning. She did not fear a knife's edge nor the piercing tip of an unforgiving spear.

Her eyes brightened as she joined the final strip to her makeshift rope. All strands of bedding, clothing and tapestry were torn and tied for this purpose: to escape, to outlive a world where no candle could burn through the lonely night.

She pulled her chair over to a small gap in the sea of stones and peered out into the waning darkness. She was ready. Out the window she climbed, carefully lowering herself down the cloth from knot to knot. She paused after seeing a heavily spotted toile—blood red. She knew she would soon reach the end.

She hovered helplessly above the moat. The rising sun would soon reveal her dangling on homemade twine. The warden and his thugs would pull her back into the vacuum of adolescence. She could not go back. She would never go back.

She closed her eyes and let go. Down and down she went, holding her breath all the way down.

Splash!

The murky water went eerily still.

Addison?

There were no bubbles breaking the water's surface.

Addison? Did she hit her head?

The sun kissed the horizon. Light spilled onto the castle walls and into the moat. Its warmth pawed at the water till Addison began to move one arm, then the other. As her head emerged, her lungs choked out more and more foul water. She coughed and smiled, coughed and smiled. Her freedom clung to her as tightly as her wet clothes.

Addison? Why did she think "Addison" as she read those pages? This story wasn't about her. She knew that. She had no desire whatsoever to be a princess. Yet this book called to her as did the childhood friends who dreamt upon its pages.

She frowned. She knew Buttons would have drowned if he hadn't stayed behind. Maybe the ending would be different this time. Could it? Could they find each other before the end? It seemed almost too much to ask. Still, hope and more hope decorated Addison's face—

A shout rang in her ears. She let go, falling backward, bouncing once before coming to rest upon her bed. As she traced the mahogany trim with the tip of her finger, she wondered how doing such a thing could make any difference. But it did. Her pain faded. She felt warm, safe. It was magical, a real gift.

Her father's voice was booming now, like the Fourth of July. She disrupted his fireworks with thoughts of fried pickles, enormous ice cream cones, cotton candy … Addison once relished that summer holiday, especially the year they celebrated at the state fair. But no more. It was too much: her mother's blinding light followed by her dad's deafening thunder. She thought she would miss visiting acres and acres of animals, until she imagined her parents' horns locked in battle, pushing each other back and forth along the kitchen floor, knocking over, crushing all manner of missiles, all manner of snaps and snakes.

Addison's parents fought all the time. They couldn't agree on where to vacation or how to spend a Sunday afternoon. Maybe that's why they were always busy with work: so that they wouldn't have to be together. They had everything and somehow it wasn't enough. Money couldn't compensate for all their differences, all their missed moments, all their volumes of unkind words.

As far as Addison knew, they only had one fight about her, about her relying too much on her looks to get what she wanted. Addison heard the whole thing from her room, even with her door closed tight, even with a blanket shoved under the door. Nothing stopped the sound from finding her.

Her father was loud—as if more decibels directly translated to more persuasive logic. He shouted how beauty was the most dangerous characteristic a person could possess. He insisted beauty was a crutch, that too many young women wasted their lives on physical bullshit instead of reading a book or studying something important. He repeated his point, even louder, to make sure there would be no rebuttal.

Of course her mother agreed a girl should grow up brave and strong, that she should find her calling and work hard to become an expert. But her father didn't listen to her mother's words; he couldn't feel her passion. A woman didn't have to choose between intelligence and beauty. She could have both. She could be the person she wanted to be: warrior and princess, professor and student. People evolve and keep evolving. Beauty wasn't dangerous. The real evil was greed, the lust for power and money. The wealthy often became overbearing or apathetic—the loudest, the most heartless, most pathetic. Her mother didn't even shout the word pathetic. Her mother didn't need to shout. Her eyes filled every square inch of their home with light and fury.

It didn't help that her mother was so dangerously beautiful or that her father was loaded, the wealthiest man in four counties, maybe five. Somehow all his investments allowed him to ignore the real truth just inches from his ruddy nose. He shouted and drank far too much. He had earned the right to his opinion and could afford the best single malt bourbons.

Yes, her mother was stunningly beautiful, but Addison's father had to realize his bride was much more than drop-dead gorgeous. They had dated for almost three years before he proposed. Maybe he was the one too focused on the surface of things; maybe he had fallen into the very trap he so despised; maybe he only knew her physically. He had married her for her beauty—he let that slip in last week's battle royale. He was lucky his wife never joined her daughter's martial arts classes; his nose would have been broken at least once.

Did it even matter which of beauty or wealth was the most likely to corrupt a person? How could it? Addison was both: both beautiful and wealthy. At least she would be wealthy when she inherited her parents' estate. As an only child, she would have it all someday—unless her parents spent their entire fortune, which was unlikely and maybe not even possible. Her mother would likely want to work another twenty years and her father would never retire. He would never willingly give up his well-deserved power. Without complete control, without an overbearing purpose, he would crumble to dust in less than a year.

Maybe her parents would be happier if they divorced. Addison frowned as she sat on her bed; she wasn't sad, not really. Her parents would choose their fates. So she too would choose for herself. Wealth? Beauty? Warrior? Princess? She was sure that princess was off the table, but maybe student would suit her for at least the next few years.

Addison laughed as she spotted the black leather jacket in her closet. At least she knew being a biker wasn't in her future. She had tried out that persona on her last birthday and killed it. She had the right attitude and the leather fit perfectly, maybe too perfectly.

Addison remembered sneaking down the stairs and out the door as the last light went out in her parents' bedroom. She was nearly invisible, dressed in black denim and a retro black leather jacket. She looked the part: a true ninja.

The closest town was a little more than two miles down this suburban artery on the corner of Main and Elm. She had only been there once before. Her father didn't condone the aging and inadequate services offered by the quaint gathering of a few shops, bookended by a gas station and a dive bar. But she wasn't here with her parents or as a daughter—no, she was a warrior, dressed to kill and headed for a safe place to try out her new self—safe in that no one she knew would ever dare set foot in that bar. This adventure would remain her little secret.

Addison nearly passed the pub before realizing she stood on the edge of town. Strange … rows of bikes lined both sides of the street and the sign above the door read "Harley's."

She waited until three women pulled up, revving their engines. She followed them inside. When her riding buddies stopped to greet one of the tables, she pealed off and sat in an open chair along the long wooden bar. Addison smothered a smile as she admired the carved graffiti. The bartender looked at her with inquisitive eyes.

"Two beers," a voice behind her chimed in.

"One beer, I'm waiting for someone." Addison was hell-bent on owning her role. She would turn down every drink, every conversation for the first thirty minutes.

The leather-clad hulk stopped cold before swinging a second leg over the stool. He shook his head with well-worn disappointment. Addison imagined he endured rejection every night of his life. He expected a poor outcome, believing everyone would reject him without an inkling of consideration. This place was bad for him, very bad. Why did his parents let him hang out in a bar?

The beer was warmer than expected. Must be tough to keep bottles cold at the rate they're being consumed. Why wasn't it sold on tap?

A second suitor approached Addison from behind. He put his hand on her right shoulder. She blocked his advance instinctively—muscle memory, burned-in movements from all those hours of defensive training. She apologized for hitting him as he retreated back to friends who were laughing hysterically. It wasn't exactly what she intended, but it worked. No one approached her for the next twenty minutes.

"What's your name?" a third contestant asked from three seats down.

Addison had forgotten to pick her code name. Addy? No, no need to leave any clues behind, though she did prefer "Addy" over the stiffer "Addison." Her parents and classmates called her Addison. Her friends? They too called her Addison. Why didn't anyone call her Addy?

"I'm Ben. What's your name?" Ben was now in the seat next to Addy. When she glanced at Ben, she saw a big number three on his chest. He was third at bat and would likely close out the first inning—though his opening line did seem quite honest and straightforward.

"Addy." Oh shit! She hadn't meant to give her real name.

"Two beers," Ben whispered as if expecting the bartender keenly awaiting his pleasure. "One for me and one for Addy." Ben slid his hand slowly along the edge of Addy's seat. "What brings you to town, Addy?"

Ben's hand found her waist. Addy leaned back and slapped him. Ben screamed. The bar erupted in laughter. Three up, three down, and rightfully so. Ben had closed out the inning in record time. Sure he entered the box well enough. He had a nice eye, took a few balls—but when he came out swinging, his hands were all over the place.

Maybe she should leave. Her break-in period was over. Break-in. Good one. She hoped she hadn't bruised Ben's cheek. Okay, okay, she should go.

"Hi," he said to Addy without looking at her—and without touching her. He seemed reasonable enough. Addy was still watching him as he turned.

Their eyes met.

"Bartender, no more beer for us tonight. How about a couple of shots?"

"No, I have to go," she said oddly as if trying to convince herself.

The shots were already in front of them. "If you leave now, I'll have to drink both—"

Addy reached for her shot and threw it down her throat. Ben couldn't move. He watched as Addy made the second one disappear in a single motion. Ben's lips parted in disbelief. She leaned-in and kissed him. A blissful smile fluttered across his face. The gawking bikers exploded in laughter. Every eye watched as she slammed the shot glass against the bar and strutted out.

The walk home seemed all up hill. It was a mistake—not that she left. She was right to leave. She had to leave. The kiss was a mistake. She knew nothing about him—other than the look in his eyes and the taste of his lips.

Addison wriggled her shoulders deeper and deeper into her bed to hide from the swath of light which cut her bedroom in two. She could hear her parents still fighting. She wished wealth would buy a knife and slay beauty—if only to put an end to their argument.

Her eyes circled the room till they reached her armoire, an antique crammed full of outgrown clothes stained by well-explored mud puddles. In the topmost drawer, she kept her favorite letter—

"The mirror!"

She shook her head violently, repeating the same gibberish over and over again, attempting to override a venomous thought, to block its very existence. But such evil cannot be silenced. Demons drip into this world between raindrops, ravage young minds, linger upon tongues.

She nearly convinced herself she was only playing a part, only pretending to be ill, when she heard her mother shout at her father.

Her mother shouted? Her mother never shouted. Addison should have been proud to hear her mother fight back, but she wasn't. She knew her parents' relationship would soon be over. She could hear her mother stomping up the stairs … in her bedroom now, probably packing her suitcase.

Sweet sixteen? It didn't feel much like a birthday. Addison raised the hourglass she created at the state fair. There was something soothing in the rhythm of the red grains falling through pinched glass. But today, maybe because she was a little older, she could see how the sands of time had a way of changing things. Sometimes the shift was so small it went unnoticed. Little by little, tick by tick—

Addison could hear her mother crying.

Time had a way of hardening one's heart. It would be another two years before Addison could venture out on her own. She didn't want to be traded back and forth between parents, but there was no escape. Their marriage wouldn't survive the hour. Grain by grain, their time was running out.

In five more minutes, Addison would face her parents. She shrugged her shoulders and buried her nose in a book. The novel felt heavy, each page struggled to turn. Her blood-red lips crimped to sobering pout. She was the one trapped in the evil castle's spire. Her pulse quickened. The air seemed too thin to breathe. All she wanted was to finish this one chapter, this one lousy chapter before breakfast—was that too much to ask?

Anger swelled inside her. She clenched her fists, squared her shoulders, hardened her gaze. She looked down her nose at her reflection. She started to count without really knowing why.

"Four," she said convincingly, then paused to look at her shoes.

"Three."

"Two." She was ready.

"One." Oddly, her steel-green eyes softened, yet their sparkle still lit the curves of her silken face. A reddish curl dropped from behind her ear, bouncing along its path before kissing her cheek.

She was doomed. Everyone would see her beauty first. Who would need more before wanting her? How could she be sure of anything in a world where she had to wrestle her own beauty for control of her destiny? Could she trust anyone?

She cringed. She could devise a set of trials to qualify worthy candidates—or just never wear makeup or tight-fitting clothes. She could comb her hair straight, cut it short, dye it crimson. No, Mom would never let her. Life just wasn't fair. She was more than her beauty, even if no one seemed to notice. She hovered. An idea began to take shape … yes, back to the mirror. She looked left and right, up and down, scanning her reflection for a flaw, something, anything that could give her hope.

Nothing. Doubt filled her mind. Was Dauphine a real friend? Did that boy in homeroom like the real Addy? Her future seemed so uncertain. A name kept echoing in her mind. Who was he? She didn't know or couldn't remember. She even felt regret for turning him away. He was the only person who really loved her—but who was he? She didn't even know anyone by that name!

Addison heard something familiar filter through her door: a few notes from an old song. Her mother was singing in the kitchen. An occasional wooden spoon against a pot filled in for a key percussion part. She listened for her mother's voice, focusing on that sweet sound tugging at her, pulling her in. The world slowed down, way down. She could feel her own heart beating slower, softer. She felt connected to something larger than herself. She was floating and so very happy. She heard a faint knocking but stayed tuned to the melody of the song. How she loved this wonderful feeling of peace. She could stay here forever—

A pebble pierced the water's surface, creating an unwelcome ripple.

Don't do that, please don't do that.

She heard laughter. The song began to speed up. The knocking grew louder and the dropping of pebbles more frequent. Still Addison refused to leave her bubble. Someone resorted to banging with both fists to get her attention.

There it was, staring back at her from the mirror. She could see it clearly now. It was a bit small, a mistake. Joy tickled her smallish nose. Addison smiled like never before. Her beauty radiated in one adorable wave after another, just like the ripples from all those pebbles. She sighed dramatically. Would her flaw be enough? Maybe not forever, but for now, it was all she needed—as long as she never smiled again.

The thunder! No, not the thunder. She turned the pages of her book quickly, searching for her favorite part—the scene where the hero found her place, her purpose:

She rose lighthearted, her face beaming, despite a sleepless night. She stood tall, shoulders square, ready. Her eyes burned as candles against the still horizon. Her hope, newborn, fragile, would soon be fueled by a thousand suns. Darkness would devour the world no more.

As Addison started down for breakfast, she heard no song, no joyful percussion on pots and pans. She could hear something faint, growing louder and louder with each step: sobbing, bursts and echoes of uncontrollable grief.

Addison stormed out without closing the front door. She meant to slam it shut, to rattle the life out of that knocker, that hang about. Why was it even there? No one knocked anymore. No one even visited.

The rising sun caught her eye. Inhaling an unusually large and purposeful breath, she crushed that joy before it could sing to her heart.

Four, three, two, one. Dragon fire snorted through flaring nostrils, burning all limbs to a crisp. Her piercing green eyes heeded the path ahead. She walked effortlessly, as if aided by wings.

Eyes forward, eyes forward. She didn't look back even though part of her could sense the new day breaking free. Even as the sun shed the last tatter of night, she would not let anything steal her anger.

She turned at the usual corner, but continued past her bus stop, maneuvering through the young men and women. Bits and pieces of their breakfast conversations filtered into her mind. Several students watched her as she slid her hips through the crowd; one whistled.

She would walk the almost two miles to school. All eyes would soon lose track of her—only ten more steps till she'd vanish round the bend.

After a few blocks, she realized her wish had come true. She was alone. No one from the bus stop had followed her, not that she expected anyone would. She wasn't even sure what she meant. Of course she hated being stuck in this town, trapped in adolescence. Everybody wanted something from her.

Ben, oh, Ben! He too was a year older now. She wanted to be free, not alone. Would he always be out of reach? After she turned eighteen, no one would be outside her grasp. Her anger was still with her, but the burning punch had faded.

Still, something weighed her down. She didn't like being hung up on anything. Ben wasn't the only name repeating in her mind. Who was he? How could she be with someone and not be forced to give up so much of herself? How could she feel this way about a man she never met?

Addison stopped. The leaves were ripe with color. She began to gather the red ones first. She could hear the school bell ringing in the distance. She was now only a stone's throw from an overly warm homeroom, overflowing with whispered lies and ogling eyes. Just a few more red ones, then the orange ones over there. A few friends would wish her a good morning. She knew that.

Geppetto's Workshop

THE construction's clangor rang a hundred hammers strong: fists clenching, pounding home, steel upon steel, ringing, again and again ringing. There could be no refuge as the cacophony swelled to feverish din, each perfunctory strike echoing from each perfunctory wall, reflecting and reflecting back again.

"Ear plugs help," the project lead offered as she introduced herself. She motioned for Adam to offer his hand. He obeyed without a word, hardly noticing how her hair rested gently along the curve of her shoulder, how her perfume, though sufficiently alluring, seemed superfluous in air thick with saw dust. He knew not to resist the will of a redheaded woman. *Resistere futilis*. It was as true in real life as it was in the movies.

Can a man and a woman be just friends?

The world is full of unmet friends. The smallest of things can spark a friendship. So, yes, a man and a woman can be just friends. Wouldn't such a theory need an actual example, an actual friend?

A sadness covered Adam's face. Truth and logic made such poor lunch companions.

Perhaps his position as an authority figure stood in the way of friendship. Would-be acquaintances would fear his power. Power? What power? He had more pock marks than power. Did even God turn His eyes from the scars of middle-age?

She dropped two very large, very soft orange cones into the palm of his right hand. She bit her lower lip as she looked deeply into Adam's hopeless eyes. She had seen this kind of shell shock before. Why do clients think they can occupy buildings under construction?

"Thank you," Adam accepted the ear plugs without looking up. He knew not to look. This wasn't his first ride on life's merry-go-round.

Civilizations have been forfeited in a mere revolution or two. Wanting hearts search and search as valiant ponies round the bend, till scouring eyes meet and meld. It can take a lifetime to break such bonds.

She suggested Adam work from home or at least find safety under his desk. She didn't care to know any details of his undisclosed governmental project. She laughed. Secrets come and go, but the hammer, the hammer lives forever.

Adam's closet-sized office gave no shelter against the storm of whirling teeth and clashing metal. He imagined a circular saw mounted to his head as he crawled under the desk. Would life really be all that different if he were cybernetic?

Life has too many questions. There isn't time to ponder if it's perfectly reasonable to fall in love while hiding under a desk. Wait. If it's your desk, in your office … why wouldn't it be reasonable?

Adam felt queasy. He put an ear plug into his left, then his right ear before squinching into a thinker's position. He took a deep breath. Surprisingly, the office really didn't seem that much smaller from this new under-the-desk point of view. To some, his five-foot-nine, two hundred pound frame might look foolish, but perceived versus actual reality was surely a matter of perspective. Others might think him spontaneous, adventurous, as he tested his assumptions while cloistered under a desk.

Adam reached up, patting the desktop till he found a stack of papers. He studied the first two pages carefully, then leafed through the next two dozen in a matter of seconds. His core ideas were solid, but soon, very soon, the physical world would challenge all of his assertions.

Think, think. Light travels in a straight line as does time. Are you sure time travels in a straight line? Does it branch at the drop of a hat or after the roulette wheel lands on a lucky number? Probably not.

Can we influence which instance of ourselves continues on path *A* and which follows the forked *B* path? Adam imagined a huge tree—a forest of trees?—with countless branches and a unique Adam on every leaf.

Adam shivered. There must be some form of self-control, some pruning of redundant branches, right? Maybe viewing time as a tree is too freeform, maybe each forked branch runs parallel to the initial branch. Maybe time is a highway—

"On-ramps? Off-ramps?"

"Don't go there."

"A lane of time isn't zero width, is it? So a little curve here and there works out fine."

"The time dimension could be infinitely wide."

"Adam, maybe time isn't a dimension at all."

"I asked you not to go there."

"Okay, but—"

"But what, Sam?"

"What if none of this conceptual stuff matters? What if the real question is how much power do we need?"

Adam knew they were on to something big, something really big. It didn't matter whether the better approach was to flex a single timeline or to create a series of ramps to interconnect two or more streams. What mattered was how they would create enough energy to alter the flow of time.

"My gut tells me it would be easier to create a little curve than a U-turn."

Adam suspected Sam was right. It seemed logical that the requirement would be less for a smaller bend. But how much power would it take?

Adam needed to get his hands dirty. He grew two inches at the thought of doing something constructive.

"Where's that little red—"

He spotted his toolbox pinned against the far side of the desk under a pile of papers detailing the original design. His concept was bold and if it worked he would go where no person had gone before. It took courage to bet on such a tiny pony. Only those who print money make such wagers.

Adam couldn't quite reach the toolbox and wasn't happy the fugitive was red. He disliked red on anything but cars, clothes, lips, leather, hair—the list of exceptions was longer than he expected. Anyway, he disliked red tools and especially little red toolboxes. Black, gray, silver: those were the colors befitting … Adam's face went blank … befitting a stodgy captain.

Still, it was an awfully small toolbox. Did it matter if it were a little blue or little red one? It wasn't worth his time to paint all his troubles blue. Adam peered into the box but couldn't spot the 13 mm wrench.

"Damn metric system," he whined as he pulled out the hammer and pipe wrench to get a better look at the remaining tools. "Why is there even a pipe wrench in this toolbox?"

Adam hated plumbing almost as much as being forced to work a particular task. He'd rather paint a box blue than tackle a plumbing nightmare. It wasn't the seemingly endless number of possible fitting combinations that bothered Adam. No, he liked playing with large working sets—and yes, joining PVC pieces was easy and way more satisfying than it should be. So why even consider the pros and cons of outlawing plumbing? Adam despised all those tight dark musty spaces where pipes and programmers seem to thrive. Let's face it: plumbing is a dangerous job, filled with twists and traps and far too many holes to plug.

Adam wrapped his right hand round a medium-sized crescent wrench. "This will do."

"You never learned to weld, did you?"

"Wasn't much call for it in computer science class, Sam."

"Seriously, admit it, you never liked copper."

"True, I don't like small coins or the really big ones for that matter. How much could the U.S. Mint save by producing only one coin?"

"I meant pipes. And, by the way, there was a new invention that you might have heard about … the debit card?"

"Then say pipes when you mean pipes."

"Adam, I get why you don't want even a handful of pennies in your pocket, but what's wrong with Susan B. Anthony?"

"She was a great person, but the coin looked too much like a quarter."

"They should have made it a different color and a little bigger."

"Not sure that would have made it any more popular."

"Funny how people so easily accept tablet-sized phones but reject the weight of a dollar coin."

Adam didn't laugh. He was too busy thinking to acknowledge Sam's point. People were odd, unpredictable. The best way to predict human outcomes was to factor in loads of self-serving behavior: greed and lust sweetened with lust and greed. In business, the terminology gets polished a bit and out comes supply and demand.

"Don't forget the shiny factor. Moths are driven to—" Sam stopped mid sentence. Adam wasn't listening. "Adam?"

"There's quite a bit of overlap."

"Okay, I'll bite."

"Power is the key to everything." Adam waved his tool like a magic wand. How a crescent wrench could wield such might was beyond Sam.

"Adam, what are you trying to say?"

Adam looked pale. He spoke slowly, more slowly with each syllable. "If we solve the power equation, everything becomes possible: interdimensional travel, time travel, immortality."

Sam suspected immortality was Adam's true motivation. As a person approaches midlife, he or she—

"Or they."

As people approach midlife, they see only the lights of the big four-oh train coming round the bend.

Adam squinted while peering out the frosted office window onto the sea of unfitted lab space. Life was too complicated and getting more so with each passing day. Adam could once recall every word ever spoken in his presence. He could replay those conversations word for word months later. Now he couldn't even remember what urgent repair required a stupid metric wrench.

A devious smile crept across Adam's face. He lifted the wrench up and down to estimate its weight. He opened his office door and looked at the far wall, at the large window foolishly proportioned for a building meant to house a secret lab. Couldn't just about anyone case this joint while hiding in the woods on the far side of the road?

"Don't do it! Don't you dare throw that wrench!"

Adam wasn't listening, but he didn't throw the wrench. It was too late—too late and too hard. It would take a mountain of mass and a lifetime of experimentation to create a single on-ramp—and even if dimensions could be connected, how would that connection point be found? Would you even know when you were on a ramp? Add more ramps and how would you navigate? How would you avoid driving in circles?

Wait. Time moved forward in a straight line. A field of some sort could bend time and keep it bent, creating an on-ramp. The concept was quite simple. With enough power, interconnections were possible. Maybe this office was as good as any to invent an infinite power source.

Adam stepped back from the door. He might have the frosted window removed, but he'd keep the nameplate section. He had no desire whatsoever to smash such panes. They were autographs of sorts. He smiled, admiring how the satin border corralled all the letters of the spirited moniker. Jean-Luc would have been proud of both the color and font choices.

Well, it wasn't exactly Adam's name; it was still the name of the previous lessee. Adam had intended to correct the name after the space took shape, when the lab was more deserving of his leadership style. Unfortunately, he neglected to include the cost of a custom nameplate in the current month's projected budget.

Adam took a deep breath. Something had to be done, but what? Adam couldn't grasp any of the threads tied to the task at hand. Maybe there was a clue hidden in one of his books, maybe his notes? Maybe he should stay in his office and sort the trash. He absentmindedly tossed the wretch back into the toolbox.

Climbing into his captain's chair, Adam stared at the glass plate, into the looking glass as it were. He was glad the current name on the door shared his initials. He only had to squint a little to trick his mind into seeing the characters in the backward string as those in his own name. Adam sat quietly, admiring his good taste. Distorted images of construction workers revved their saws, fired their nail guns. It would all come together very soon. Adam was sure of it.

Months later ...

Only Adam knew about the early morning trial. Though the project wasn't ready for such an aggressive move, he had to take the risk. He needed a win even if he hadn't met any of the prerequisites, even if he hadn't earned the right to hope for such victory.

After getting up to pee for a third time, Adam dressed quickly and snuck off to work. The drive seemed an eternity. Turning on the radio as a distraction never crossed his mind. He had forgotten how to live his life. He had lost track of hobbies, lost track of friends. He now focused all his energy on a single point. Today's sunrise would ignite his dreams. But unlike a childhood magnifying glass which risked a few ants, this new and unpredictable energy circuit could torch all souls.

The lab was dark as Adam entered his access code. The hairs on the back of his neck were on end. He saw himself as the expendable character in a slasher movie, the one who insisted on going down to the basement to see what was making that eerie noise. Adam slapped his face to bring himself back to reality. He could do this—even if he couldn't, he was going to try.

He flicked on the lights. The lab came alive as his baby slept quietly in the center of his world. He patted SAM on the back.

"We got this."

His kinship spoke a miraculous and painful truth about Adam. He cared far too deeply for his creation, this complex set of mathematical energy converters encased in shiny metal. He walked over to the electrical panel and switched on the last remaining circuit. His child's eyes filled with light.

Adam noted the date and time in the lab journal before initiating the trial. With his attention riveted to the output gauge, he marveled as the power grew linearly—just as he predicted! The available energy was already at forty percent and still climbing.

A vibration warning light flashed on. Adam looked carefully at SAM, his chassis, his connectors, but saw nothing out of the ordinary.

"Fifty, fifty-five." He would shut down at seventy percent. He lifted the safety cover off the kill switch and readied himself.

"Sixty." The power conduit shook ever so slightly before a massive surge lifted SAM off the floor. The overhead tubing shifted abruptly, breaking free of its supports. Adam tried to engage the kill switch, but it was too late. An intense energy wave shot from the end of the power conduit, wiping out the far back wall.

"The log!" It would take weeks to rebuild the lab, but all would be forgiven if the log clearly showed the accumulated energy curve. Adam could generate a series of charts to depict how the energy level grew over time, demonstrating how predictably the energy generation circuitry had performed. Explaining the lab repairs would be a challenge ... though labeling the chart "Sonic Cannon" would lock in the next wave of investment.

Why was the console so sluggish? Why was the log not accessible? Not found, bullshit. It's there. Just go and get it. Adam started a series of diagnostics to check SAM's core.

The screams of a half dozen firetrucks woke many miles of neighbors. Dozens of brave men and women would soon break through the lab's front door if he didn't stop now to let them in. No log. No results yet on the diagnostics.

Adam pushed the front door open. Once the crews were inside, the excitement died quickly as little could be done. There was no fire. The electricity along the missing wall had shut off automatically. With vacant spaces on three sides of the building, SAM got lucky, spilling his guts across mostly barren land.

Before heading out, the fire company shut off the water supply to avoid future complications. They warned Adam he'd have to pay for repairs out of pocket since he had a hand in the accident. He'd need to sweet-talk the insurance company if he hoped to keep his policy. And he'd have to pay for clean-up and replacement of about a dozen trees in the neighboring lot. Not so barren on that side after all.

Adam thanked the brigade for coming and especially for leaving. He needed to get back to work. As the last fighter left, she suggested Adam get his head checked. Was she being sarcastic? In any case, there wasn't time. He had to get back to the diagnostics and prepare those charts.

Adam's heart skipped a beat. The first diagnostic test failed as did the second and third—SAM failed all his tests. Bad SAM, bad SAM. For all intents and purposes, he was dead.

"Pile of shit!"

Entropy Sucks

YESTERDAY, Adam's life seemed perfect, almost flawless, as sturdy as a well-bound book. He focused on a clean start: each page cut carefully to exacting standards, each paragraph clearly on one page or the next, never a stranded line at the top or bottom, no, never a stranded line. By all accounts, he had done that part fairly well, exceedingly well—in fact, far more duly with each retelling of the story.

Yet, life ebbs. A peak can come and go in a matter of minutes. You're over that sugary hill before your tongue can appreciate its sweetness. Whereas a valley, a valley likes to linger; its bitterness settles low in your throat, often a bit too low. Some might need a push to get off the couch.

Adam was such a person. After a few typos in his early twenties and a confusing scene here and there, a melancholy settled along the floor of Adam's apartment. He needed someone to help write his second chapter. His recently graduated heroine was ready to begin a new life….

The moon hung precariously, held against the hazy night sky by a single push pin. They stopped at a corner. Adam was nervous. She might say no. He reached into his pocket and opened the box. Their future fell from his fingers. A nearby streetlight didn't help. Even their shadows obscured the ring. A mist rolled in. Was he dreaming?

He felt with his hands. The pine needles were very dry with many prickly ends. As Wendy knelt to aid the search, the gem revealed itself. They both were still on their knees. Her eyes were intense, so perfectly green, adorned with flecks of pure gold. She was the real treasure.

Why hadn't she said yes? Was something wrong?

He hadn't asked. "Will you—"

Her yes came quickly. She might have been bluffing if her lips weren't so soft, if her kiss didn't press on and on, if the fireworks weren't so spontaneous, so impressive.

Adam smiled. He did okay. He might have said "if you don't mind" one or two too many times, but he had done this one thing well enough that the rest of his pages seemed to write themselves. Each new chapter brought new wonders. Within five months, they were married and living in upstate New York. Wendy landed a permanent job as a hospital caseworker just a few miles from where Adam worked as a development programmer. Money wasn't an issue for the first time in Adam's life.

Adam wasn't traveling much, though the regular sessions with an out-of-state partner would soon ramp up. So for at least the next few months, the couple would commute to work together. Adam would drive. Wendy wouldn't. She couldn't. She didn't have a driver's license, a coming-of-age milestone her parents intentionally overlooked.

Every family has stories, but the tale which ended all driving lessons in Wendy's family was legendary. After Wendy's parents were married, her mother wanted to learn to drive. Some skills are hard to grasp and maybe with all the complexity, all the danger involved with driving a moving vehicle, things can heat up quite easily. Shortly after getting her permit, the student driver got pregnant with twin boys. Twins. Fast forward a few years, the boys were now busy with school, so why not try again? The student secured another learner's permit which again drove things to get all hot and bothered. Bingo! Second permit, second pregnancy. One must learn to read the fine print. When he heard they were expecting again—this time, a girl—Father was speechless. All he could manage was: "No more learner's permits." Wendy's mother did eventually get her driver's license, at age seventy-six. Seemed like a safe thing to do.

So, you can see why Adam took his responsibility so seriously. Oh, he would teach her every evening, every weekend—every waking moment if he could, if she would let him. Wendy passed the driving tests but not before she too got pregnant.

The soon-to-be parents were clueless but had good instincts. Their first child would want for nothing. He or she would learn to run fast, play baseball, and blow sweet notes on a silver trumpet. Life was perfect. By the end of page twenty-three, Adam was married. A page later, he would be a proud father, nearing promotion.

Yes, the paid overtime would end—not the overtime, just the time-and-a-half pay. Even with the raise, Adam was just given a forty percent pay cut and the amount of required travel more than doubled. The now salaried employee would soon support the newly released product round the globe. Money again was a problem and that summer was especially warm. It might have made a good story if Adam had time to tell it.

Money grew short as the summer stretched on. Her life seemed somehow paused: a reflection in the shoppe window. Sweat dripped from her brow. She imagined the flavor perfecting as the taffy pulled thinner ... oh, so thin ... such strawberries would melt in her mouth.

No loitering. It was a stupid sign. What else would a pregnant woman do in front of a candy store?

It would be her first child. Life was hard, so very hard. She needed a drink, a cool spot to sit and think. Maybe she should head back; her husband would be home soon. She laughed. Maybe he sold his guitar and bought an air conditioner for the living room.

The flight back from Japan would be fourteen of the longest hours in history. He would survive. He always survived. Was there any other choice? Adam laughed. He would sell his guitar. It was an unbearably warm summer.

Adam's smile attracted attention. Everyone seemed to want to talk with him. When one of the flight attendants learned he was returning to his bride after a ten-day business trip, she bumped him up to first class and offered him a bottle of champagne to celebrate his homecoming. Adam appreciated the champagne; he really did, though the bottle might never get opened. Wendy quit drinking the moment she thought she might be pregnant.

"It's a girl!"

Joy burst out across Wendy's face as the pain stopped, as she raised her arms to hold her baby. "How are you so little when you were gigantic just a minute ago?"

Sarah smiled back at her mother.

"It's probably gas." Adam stroked his daughter's head and started counting. Ten fingers, ten toes. When could they take her home?

Nothing was more important than this child. She was their world before she took her first breath.

Adam woke, still on the plane, still hours from touchdown. He had been dreaming about his perfect life, a life he attributed to Wendy—and now to children too. He had spent his free time shopping for gifts. Would they like the oriental outfits? Would the toy train be too loud?

He fell asleep before the end of the next movie. He was back at college, sitting in his dorm room. Incomplete work piled high on a tiny desk. He needed to stretch his arms, but he couldn't without hitting the wall to his left or the built-in armoire on his right. The sun was bright, the room exceedingly warm. A little fresh air would have been wonderful.

Adam wiped his brow. He took a deep breath, then another. He looked out the oversized dorm window—or was it the airplane window? Everything went black. He didn't know where he was. He wasn't even sure of his age. Was he nineteen? Twenty-five? Thirty-nine?

"Addy? Is that you?"

"Not cool, dude. Not cool."

"Sam?"

"Open your eyes."

Adam peeked. The light was too bright. "Sam, where are you?"

"Where I always am."

Adam frowned. Where had the last twenty years gone? His self-image hadn't aged despite fleeting glances to check for mussed hair … until this morning, when he stared too long into the looking glass. Was that nose now a bit wider? That jaw line a little spongy? Adam poked along his jaw in disbelief. Who was this pale and sluggish man whose face was marred with spots?

Something snapped. Adam's life fast-forwarded from nineteen to thirty-nine. He was not unattractive or unimportant. He was both. What could he do? Long term, stay the course, though he could get elected to congress and sponsor a bill against reflective surfaces. In the short term? Affair or sports car?

"Maybe both."

Why not? The kids were grown and mostly self-sufficient. His wife had part-time work and more than enough friends to fill her— Adam stopped midthought, remembering yesterday as he was leaving for the office….

She stopped him, grabbed him by the shoulder, spun him round. They were standing face to face. An intoxicating warmth radiated from her body. Her dreamy eyes seemed as pools of wonder. He could feel her soul. She plucked a string from his shoulder and wished him farewell.

All life drained from his face. He looked down at the string. It was now a string of a totally different color. Had he used work to escape a life that lost its spark? Adam studied his shoes. Something had to change. Yes, something had to change; but no, he was not going to shine those shoes.

"Divorce? Change jobs? Sell the kids?"

"Divorce is expensive. Fifty percent of couples get divorced, but how many recover financially?"

"Right, who wants to work into their seventies?"

"I have a friend who got divorced. He drove his car into the ground while waiting for someone to show him some serious interest. So no divorce, thank you very much."

"Sell the kids?"

"Well, it's all about the timing. The kids have grown up so fast: innocence has faded, boundaries are tested hourly."

"Honestly, Adam, kids are like veal. Your only chance to sell them is when they're young. Just kidding. Not really. You can sell them at any age—if they're cute."

"They are, but there might be some significant obstacles, like love and a number of well-enforced laws."

"So, career?"

"Career it is. We'll start fresh as soon as my proposal gets approved."

"What was our pitch called?"

"'Sustainable Meta-energy to Fuel Scientific Research—'"

"'And Beyond!' Don't forget that last part was my idea."

Sam entered without knocking.

"Get out. I'm a serious scientist. I no longer give art lessons."

"I read that entry."

"Go away. Take Your Kid To Work Day isn't till next week."

"Take Your Kid To Work Day is in April."

It wasn't April?

"I read that entry."

"What entry?"

"Adam, I think you meant 'which' entry."

"What?"

"Which!"

Adam forgot all the mountains he could not move. "Sam, please don't start any witch hunts."

"Who are you calling a witch?"

"Who's a witch?"

Sam laughed. He knew where Adam was heading. "Who's a baseball player."

Adam's face soured. That wasn't the right line—and Sam should have feigned confusion. Was Adam so troubled that even first-rate comedians weren't enough? "Sam, I don't have time for this."

"But your journal entry—"

"Fine. It's a lab journal, not a personal journal."

"I don't know, Adam. It sounded kinda personal."

"Third base."

"Okay, now you're avoiding the subject." Sam paused just long enough to raise his right eyebrow. "And anyway, when's the last time you made it to third base?"

"Sam, this isn't a real conversation and you know I haven't played baseball in years."

"Right, softball was your game. Get it?"

"No, I don't get it and I don't want it, especially not from you. We're not having this conversation and I haven't played softball in years." Adam plugged his ears with his fingertips.

"Déjà vu."

"What?" Adam showed more concern for what was on Sam's mind now that he couldn't hear a word. Sam motioned for Adam to remove his fingers, then burst out laughing as Adam seemed genuinely confused about how his stubby fingers found their way into his ears. When, Sam wondered, when did Adam's fingers get to be that stubby?

Something snapped. Adam's stubby fingers? Sam laughed and laughed. He couldn't stop laughing. "Déjà," he struggled to speak, "déjà vu!"

"Sam, stop repeating yourself." A childish joy returned to Adam's aspect. "There's only one 'déjà' per 'vu' and you can't say things like that. I'm the one who says things like that."

"Oh, okay," Sam shook his head side to side and looked very woozy. "Now I feel like we're stuck in some kind of time loop. Adam, please stand still."

"Seriously, Sam?"

Sam stopped laughing. He looked Adam squarely in the eyes. "Adam, if you want to be serious, then tell me what you meant by that journal entry!"

"Entropy sucks."

"Adam, you're such an enigma."

"I'm so glad you said that!"

"You're glad I called you a noncommunicable introvert?"

"Yes, of course, but I think you meant non-communicative."

"Adam, if you don't stop the subterfuge—"

"OK, Sam, but first let me say two things. *A*, I'm so glad I'm an enigma because that means you can't read my mind. And secondly, and more importantly, why is it that 'non-communicative' needs a hyphen but 'noncommunicable' does not?"

"Can we get back to our discussion about your death?"

"This isn't a discussion and I never 'died' to my knowledge."

"Stop stalling and tell me what you meant by 'death of original thought' … or else!"

"OK, wait a minute. I haven't written a journal entry on that topic … but if I had, I know what I would've said." Sam's eyes glazed over. "Look, Sam, the landscape is changing rapidly. Soon it will be impossible to do anything truly unique."

"You're losing me."

"Everything has already been said, everything has already been done—at best we can translate into current-day language. Soon, it won't matter what we think, say or do. Everything we invent, everything we hold dear can vanish in an instant. We won't even remember ever having—"

"Adam, English, please."

"It won't matter who invents time travel first."

"Since someone can go back in time and steal it?"

"Exactly! Kill off the inventor, go back earlier in time and 'precreate' the later invention. Any number of scenarios wreck the original timeline."

"Hey, this time travel stuff is pretty cool."

"No, it's a nightmare. The deadly sins will conquer our souls."

"Our souls … deadly sins … all seven of them?"

"Maybe, but mostly the triple threat of pride, greed and envy."

"Not lust? I'm a big fan of lust."

"Of course you are. You think everything is about sex."

"Sex or love. But don't force us off topic. Let's get back to that whatchamajig."

"Name one thing humans haven't corrupted. Time travel would be no different. It would be the cause of the next war: to own exclusive control of the technology. Anything that can be accomplished can be undone or replaced. No one would be allowed any unsanctioned thought. They will be everywhere, lurking in the shadows, ready to erase all traces of anyone who dares to invent, dares to disobey. People will fear all creative thought."

"Yeah, they would lurk, wouldn't they? So, no more of this, no more of that … no more poetry?"

"Right, Sam. No more poetry."

Sam suppressed his desire to smirk. He was really starting to see the silver lining in this time travel dilemma. He could console Adam, but wouldn't it be better to be the one in control and change Adam's dream to be something less controversial? Adam could be a decent plumber, if he worked at it. He had the necessary attributes. His pants hadn't fit for at least the last ten years.

Yes, Sam would be happy to be the first to invent time travel if only to kill off poetry. Sam turned his head to hide the sparkle escalating in his eyes. He could barely contain his overwhelming desire to be a scientist. The world domination part was gravy—and a burden, a difficult but welcomed burden for sure. Not that gravy is a burden, unless you have to make it from scratch.

Sam tired of the immense weight thrust upon his shoulders. Maybe he should be the one to invent the lock on the machine. He would own the only key.

"Sam?"

"Yes, Adam?"

"One more thing. No more premium TV channels."

The light went out in Sam's eyes. Entropy really does suck.

Without another word, they knew what they had to do.

A Toast to Sam

ADAM arrived first and requested a booth in the back corner of the bar. He ordered two *weiße Biere*, knowing Sam would be along shortly. The waitress seemed oddly amused, lingering unexpectedly. She didn't say anything but kept smiling, kept watching his every move. Adam bit his lower lip as he rocked in his seat. If she were waiting for him to say—

"Is it hot in here?" Adam blurted out as he loosened his tie. He usually wore casual clothes, but his first face-to-face sponsor meeting had just ended and he couldn't have faced that crowd underdressed.

She leaned in, shifting her weight to her left hip, resting her left palm on his table.

"Much warmer in Raleigh than in New York," Adam offered.

She straightened her elbow and rolled her right shoulder forward. "You from NYC?" Her eyes were still locked on Adam's baby blues.

People sure were friendly in the South. She was likely in her early thirties, though most folks might think her twenty-nine. She was at her ideal weight and maybe had recently gained a few pounds as her clothes fit a bit tight. Her work shift had just started, so she probably wasn't fidgeting because of tired legs or sore feet. Was she expecting him to say something in particular?

She leaned over the table and touched his hand.

"No, upstate. Can we get those beers in the half-liter glasses, the tall ones?"

"Sorry, can't join you; against house rules." She turned and was gone.

"We're officially moving to Pennsylvania when the lab is ready," Adam continued, speaking each subsequent word more slowly and more softly, whispering the last word to himself.

"But I can join you," Sam said as he took his place at the table. He too wanted to have a serious discussion about time travel.

"Two wheat beers." The glasses were barely down before the waitress spun around and strutted away.

Sam put his index finger against the lip of his glass to steady it. "Wheat or white?" Sam watched her hips move left, right, left, right. "What did you say to piss off such an attractive woman?" Adam glared at Sam. "Tell me, Adam, what did you do?"

"Made with wheat; literally 'white'; nothing: I think she expected me to order food."

Sam raised his glass to make a toast. "Anyway, first things first, when in Rome—"

"Germany, really. *Weizenbier* is 'wheat' beer."

Sam took a big swig. It was good. White foam covered his upper lip. "I love 1040."

"Oldest brewery in the world."

"Draft, right?"

"Yes, draft is better." After a long awkward pause, Adam checked his watch.

"What time is it?"

"It's barely after four, but it's after five somewhere."

"Enough, Adam! Why don't we just use a particle accelerator? It's proven technology."

"Yes, it works, but it has its quarks."

"Did you say quirks or quarks?"

"Quarks. It's hard to isolate quarks."

"Yeah, they are a bit clingy—"

"More like clumpy. And the last thing we want is to have to clean up all those broken strings."

"Right … broken strings." Sam put his left hand round his chin, pretending to understand quark confinement. "Free quarks have always been suppressed."

"Exactly!" Adam waved at the waitress to get her attention. "I'll show you."

"Adam, don't! She's way out of your league."

"Nonsense."

When the unhappy waitress returned, Adam asked for two bottles of her best domestic beer. Sam finished his *Hefeweizen* and sat with great anticipation. The two bottles arrived in less than thirty seconds. Sam grabbed one of the lagers and started to drink.

"Stop, put it down." Adam tapped the bottom of his bottle against the top of Sam's. Sam's bottle overflowed, spilling all over the table and onto the floor.

"Adam! You capped my beer!"

Adam didn't answer. He couldn't take his eyes from the uncontrollable frothing consequences of his actions.

"Give me your napkin. Adam!"

Adam sat locked in place. Sam had seen Adam like this before. Scanning the bar, Sam found no redheads, not even a woman in a red dress. If Adam wasn't overwhelmed by the presence of a redheaded woman, then … he must be doing complex calculations in his head.

Adam began to smile as his eyes darted from the spilled beer to the ceiling and back to the floor. "It's a series of waves,"

"No, it's a freaking mess!"

"Yes, a freaking mess and a series of small waves which break up the bubbles … look at all those bubbles!"

"All dressed up and no where to go."

"Exactly, Sam!"

"What?"

"They need somewhere to go … but even when the waves make them freak out, the collateral damage is only spilt beer and a few paper towels."

"What a waste." Sam shook his head. "I could have chugged that beer. How much is left in the bottle?"

"About five ounces."

"Which is how many milliliters?"

"147."

"How did you know that?"

"Sam, I think the better question is why didn't you know that."

"Not so fast, you mathematician, you."

Adam smiled. He enjoyed Sam's complimenting and teasing him at the same time.

"Do you think in milliliters or did you convert?"

"Convert."

"And?" Adam reached for a napkin and wrote "(n fl. oz. x 30) - 2%." "Seriously, you know a heuristic for fluid conversion?"

"Again, Sam, the better question—"

"Stop. You're lying. I know your tell." Adam covered his face. "Adam, give it up."

"There's a five ounce tube of hand cream in the second drawer of my desk."

"Right or left?"

"Right side."

Sam smiled. His poker skills were expanding into the real world. He chugged those last five ounces with great joy.

Adam's eyes widened. "Sam, that's it! Fast gulps, wide straw … no … no … tiny straw!"

"But then the bubbles would accelerate and make an even bigger mess."

"Right, more mess or at least more risk of more mess."

Sam smiled. "More risk, more reward."

"Control the path round the doughnut … hold the bending curve … speed of light."

"Careful, Adam, don't drink and fold space-time."

"We need a single atom black hole … in a tiny straw!"

"A baby wormhole?"

"Yes … yes … no. I mean, we might end up creating a wormhole—which would be really cool—but first we need somewhere for all that excess gas to go. We want the distance between dimensions to approach zero, but we don't want to create any uncontrolled interdimensional collisions."

"Okay, I see where you're going. We just need a thin curvy straw with a single atom black hole overflow pipe?"

"Yes."

"Yes? I'm right? Wow, write that in your journal: 'Sam invented all the key—'"

"Sam, don't joke around! Continue your thought … curvy straw … is that one curve or a series of—"

"This kinda reminds me of that *Star Trek* movie where there are two Spocks, a young one and an old one."

"Sam, you'll have to be more specific. Spock was reborn in one movie and time traveled in at least one other."

"No, not the Genesis one, the one where time moves slower near the…."

"Singularity. Time moves slower near a singularity than on the orbiting planets. So singularity Spock stays about the same age while the other Spock ages a few decades."

"Right, so we're looking for a singularity?"

"Yes, Sam, a singularity."

"And we want to avoid any rocket-type behavior or explosions?"

"Yes, no booms."

"And we need to keep the black hole from expanding and sucking all existence through a thin curvy straw?"

"Yes."

"Can you say anything besides yes?"

"Yes, though I'm not sure how to account for the gravitational waves."

"I knew there'd be a showstopper. Tell me again about the old-school particle acceleration alternative."

"Sam, there can be no significant reward without significant risk."

"I would have said, 'With great power, comes great responsibility.'"

"Voltaire said that, right?"

"No, duh. Uncle Ben."

"So minute rice cornered the high-end power market?"

"No, dude, you're thinking about the wrong Uncle Ben … but we are cooked, aren't we?"

"Yes, so let's concentrate. If we focus our energy—"

"Can we at least include a kill switch?"

"A kill switch?"

"Adam, you know … a big black button that drops a silver ball on a track that hits a block that taps the next block and so on. I've seen hundreds of really cool videos."

"Right … and one of the blocks triggers a mechanism that pulls a cord that redirects the excess pressure through a whistle."

"Huh, seriously, you want an armageddon whistle? Totally not necessary, dude, since the blocks will reverse direction and flow backward to the starting point."

"I've seen it both ways, but the whistle is cooler."

"Okay, so we've reached an impasse. How do we know which technology is the right one?"

"Sometimes the simplest method is best. Let's throw out all the complex theories and look to nature for a comparable solution."

"So, let me get this right. You're saying you science people just sit around in bars at four p.m., making up all kinds of shit and then blame any subsequent failures on nature."

"Yes. The best scape goats are those who can't possibly defend themselves."

"So we scientists blame our failures on beer and doughnuts?"

"Yes, beer and doughnuts … and a straw, a singularity, and a whistle."

"Okay, we're all set then. How do we create a singularity?"

"Sam, no problem. I'll just pick one up from the local electronics store on my way to work tomorrow."

"I do love solving world-class problems. Is it too early for dinner? Should we order food? Hey waitress!"

The air was thick with danger. Sam struggled to rise, to take up arms against his foe. His frame would not straighten, his fists now too frail for the sword. Summoning all his might, he could not forge a shadow of a weapon. Had he lived a life prostrate to another's will, to all things towering beyond a pole or perch?

Yes, for he feared all these things: the birds, the bees, even the stronger-willed shrubberies. His eyes swam in his head. He could see only blurs of those flying creatures. A single voice, then dozens, hundreds—thousands—joining a cawing chorus, a deafening din. His anguish anchored his feet to the ground.

Halos blinded Sam. Pins and needles nailed him to his island. He pounded his left foot, then his right. Both stung badly. He made a face which would have brought tears to his mother's eyes.

The birds circled wildly overhead. Vultures he thought but didn't panic. He remained calm, too calm for all the weight resting on this moment. He was about to take his first step and no cameras were rolling. No photo, no war-hurried sketch, no oil painting would mark this occasion. He was alone. In some ways, he had always been alone. He hadn't worried about the future, hadn't considered all the complexities of life, thrust as he was into the middle of things. He hadn't even eaten yet.

Sam tested his legs again, then ventured one step forward. Despite his obvious awkwardness, he was walking. He was walking!

On his second step, he tripped over a stick, a stupid bamboo stick, and fell forward onto his stomach. The force of the fall knocked the wind out of him. He squirmed for a few seconds as though he were trying to doggy paddle. Then he stopped, completely stopped. He would gladly lie a lifetime if for no other reason than lying in a puddle was altogether different from sitting in one. He smiled out of sheer joy, then again for the irony. Falling over a walking cane might prevent him from taking the next step in his long-awaited journey.

It wasn't as if the real-life Sam lacked all ambition, he simply refused to engage in any situation which might hint at real danger. He preferred to read about courage and chivalry than to stand in a musty old cave and face the dragon. Even if he had the most "bestest" sword known to humankind, he would not care to venture into such dark or deleterious places. An extra inch of bath water would cause him to drain the tub. Whispers about snakes or spiders would force retreat. Danger was definitely not his middle name. Sam feared the dark, most clowns, and anyone or anything with the courage or depravity to hide in dimly lit corners or bedroom closets.

He could have drowned in all this sorrow, but he didn't. Reading buoyed his sanity, gave him a kind of limitless power where he could teleport to any of a countless number of worlds. The more he read, the taller his dreams grew. He could do anything, be anyone …

though he did sometimes end up in the oddest places: an upside-down planet inhabited by thousands of bats, an underwater city built entirely of pharaonic porcelain tea cups, a thin limb of an ancient oak so high above ground that it was hard to breathe and far too quiet to think. Apparently not all *M*-class planets are all that livable.

"What's next?" He shuffled through the pile flanking his bed. The feel of the physical books restored his raison d'être. His eyes sparkled as he scooped up the treasure. He assessed the gem with his left, then right hand. The book was the perfect weight for a sci-fi novel.

He enjoyed reading quickly if only so he could touch the corner of the next page as soon as possible. This tactile anticipation gave him great hope, not only for the fate of the characters in the book but for how his own future might turn out. How could any crisis be resolved without turning a page?

Occasionally, Sam would pause to absorb a sentence which spoke to him. He lived for those moments. He'd underline such a passage if only to make it more apparent to the next reader. Some students might never graduate without the aid of a good teacher—not that Sam was much of a teacher. He was more of a soldier, pushing through all manner of pages thick with brush and booby-traps. Sam laughed. He lived for words like booby-trap. No one ever got slapped for saying booby-trap. He could have said peril or pitfalls, but where's the fun in that? It wouldn't have even been alliteral.

Yes, Sam was a good soldier, a good soldier and a good fish. The back and forth of an interesting story line enticed him as simple native bait might lure even the most suspicious creature. He was hooked. He could breathe under water. He could race through the water's surface and fly and fly and fly. Flying was the best, next to skipping stones. Sam could skip stones for hours. He'd even skip on Mars if Mars had lakes.

As he turned the page, taffy-thick vermillion stretched recto over verso, pulling thin to whispery veins of carmine. Fingers of summer spread across acres of red rock, tickling out nuances of color. It seemed a sad thing to come this far and not linger in the moment, but there wasn't enough time or enough oxygen. As it was, he would have to run part of the way. He laughed, knowing he looked foolish leaning so far forward, leap-skipping like a two-legged frog. His space-suited body bounced so much at a mere 0.376 g. How the planet's surface blurred into the carbon dioxide atmosphere startled him at first. He soon learned to close his eyes on the way up and only dare to take in the sights as he glided back down. Though not his primary mission, he mentally logged nearly four hundred and eighty-two subtle variants of reddish hue. Then, when the temperature dropped enough, each sample dulled to an obviously new shade. He would tell his friends, anyone who would listen really, that he observed at least a thousand unique reds on Mars.

It was nearly nightfall before he found this world's first wonder. He scanned the once mythical lake, smiling as innocently as a wide-eyed child. He could feel a numbing cold creeping from the now nearly bluish rock. He absentmindedly rubbed his hands together. He could now report 1001 red variants.

Only a handful of minutes remained. His oxygen was low and the lake's edge had begun to crystalize. All life would soon freeze over. He searched the ground for a flat stone, not too big, not too small. He counted eight, maybe nine skips before the stone disappeared into the distance. He didn't know how far the lake stretched or if the stone was still skipping once it leaped over the horizon.

He loved how the ripples textured the water's surface. They were visual representations of the sounds only fish and turtles could hear. Snakes? Snakes don't hear like we do, but they can sense vibrations. Sam prayed for no snakes in the lake. He would be reluctant to revisit this moment if there were snakes in lakes on Mars. He laughed. Sam had substituted the name of each planet for Mars, but none rhymed with lakes, though Uranus had an interesting ring to it.

"No!" The ripples were gone. It was hard to love something that disappeared without saying goodbye.

Yet, he did. He hoped the last ripple still echoed under the water, that the fish would remember how the rock touched their lives. He could still remember the last great line he read, though it probably didn't sound like a skipping stone to a trout or sunfish. No, the rhythm wasn't a slapping, like a bass drum pounding and slowly fading to whisper. It was more like rain on a hot roof, on a hot tin roof.

Sam leaned his head way back and glared at the ceiling. He was angry with himself for thinking "tin." No one jumps to cats when they think roof or hot roof, but add "tin" and there you are. One cat, two cats—a mind full of cats … on the roof, the hot tin roof. They were mewing and mewing. They didn't like how their paws burned.

Sam sneezed. He knew he would. He was allergic to cats. He would hold his breath until he got the last cat down—before it might rain. Wet cats were the worst. He wasn't much for cats on or off the roof, wet or dry. Sam smirked. He was pretty sure he didn't like any story where the main character was a pig or a spider or any talking animal really. It just wasn't believable. Skipping stones on Mars—now that was believable. Sam was sure it would happen someday.

Sam replayed his favorite scene from last night. The rain tapped till the sun broke through the clouds. A reluctant hero woke more willing, more able to hear the true bell, to accept the path ahead.

Sam woke with a faded orange taste on his lips. He was surprised it was still dark outside and even more astonished to find himself inside. No sign of his glasses. The clock read 5:01, but he wasn't sure if it was a.m. or p.m. Had he slept almost a full day? Maybe. He felt well rested and wide awake. He tried to piece together what had happened in the last eight to twenty hours. Something was off, but he couldn't quite put his finger on what made him feel so uneasy. Had he dreamt the curtains were a different color and not this pale shade of green? The hair on the back of his neck started screaming. He spun around, expecting to see someone or something. Was he being watched?

"Breathe, breathe." Sam searched the small hotel room to convince himself he was alone. He saw no signs of an intruder and the other bed hadn't been slept in. "Flying Solo," he half-joked, half-grimaced before his eyes latched on something familiar, something miraculous: three baby oranges in a mesh bag and a half-empty bottle of water standing guard over the tiny treasures.

The easy-to-peel fruit was gone before he realized he had taken the first bite. As he swallowed the last mouthful of water, he looked long and hard at the door leading out of his room. He wondered what might be waiting for him on the other side. Friend or foe? He had no clue. He was sure of only one thing: he needed a shower.

Sam gasped as cold water struck his sun-soaked body. He squeezed his eyes shut, tighter and tighter, not expecting the temperature shock to be so overwhelming. His head throbbed as the tempest repeatedly stung his neck and chest. He fumbled to find the knob to raise the temperature as he pushed his mouth out of the waterfall to steal a breath.

How long had he been in the sun? He reached to catch a memory-drop of the warming deluge. The allusive texture escaped his innocent thumb and forefinger. Water pooled on the cool tile floor. His nostrils flared. He could smell chlorine. Did that odor emanate from the tap water or was it an association triggered by—

"Who cares? It's still way better than typhoid."

Sam took a deep breath and another. His pulse began to slow. Words started to form in his mind as the knot in his chest softened. Names of people and places danced on the tip of his tongue as the water pitter-pattered over his aching shoulders.

"It's not chlorine. Chloramines cause that pool smell." Sam knew that trivia to be fact but not how he knew something so useless. He turned the shower off and stepped out. Waves of heat radiated from his body, misting up the bathroom mirror. As he reached for the towel, he stopped. His face looked as if his puppy just died.

"Where's the goddam towel?" Sam stood motionless for nearly a minute before realizing he was not sure what to do next. Everything seemed so complex, so impossible. He was naked and alone. How could he possibly get through this without help? He lifted his foot and placed it forward purposely as if guided by an unseen force.

"No!" He stopped cold with clenched fists. He recognized his movements as some sort of dancing, as something called the "Hokey Pokey." He was in trouble and he knew it. He would have to take things one step at a time. He bit his lip as he put one foot in.

It happened over and over again. He would do a silly thing, which he had no business doing, then in the next moment forget how to do an everyday task. Why were trivial things so hard? Which sock goes on first, left or right? Why would it matter? Both were dirty leftovers.

Sam's head throbbed. What ungodly concoction had he stumbled upon yesterday—or was that earlier this morning? Even Father Time was a dick. "Enough!" He knew it was a mistake to let anyone, even himself, maybe especially himself, wander into these woods. "Look, best case, you find a chocolate house. Otherwise, you're knee-deep in poison ivy in the goddam woods."

Goddam. Goddam woods. Goddam what's-his-name. Hallelujah! He remembered! But what's-his-name was a fictional character. Sam scratched his head. Who was that guy who identified with that prep school dropout? Sam sat on a very small chair, arranging himself into a thinking pose. "Did his name start with an *R*?" Sam pounded his fist. "Focus, focus." The name he was looking for started with an *A*.

Alistair? He didn't know an Alistair. Albert? He knew a fictional Albert … but … why was his head full of snakes? Asps? Fear took hold. Sam jumped onto his bed, looking down at the carpet as if it slithered. He needed a torch.

Sam laughed as the moment's ridiculousness shook him from his nightmare. It felt good to laugh. He wished he could give the gift of laughter to everyone he met. Maybe tilting at such windmills was worse than the windmill itself.

"Think, think." Sam kept flipping between scenes of some yellow bear and a guy with a whip and cool hat. But think all he would, all he could, all he knew for sure was—

"I hate snakes." Of course he did. It's instinctual to despise something that can kill you with a single bite.

How did this day begin? Sam closed his eyes. He could see the sun burning through a canopy of sanguine leaves … how one leaf fell … did it choose its path? It was a sad memory, despite how the branches swayed like a mother's arms rocking a newborn.

Sam's heart skipped a beat. He knew he was out of his element, naive to the many truths of the physical world. He had to remind himself to see things as they really were, to believe in himself and trust those around him.

Yep, nonsense, even for a time traveler or whatever Sam's life was destined to be.

"Do I dare?" A smile burst out across Sam's face as his mind now locked on food, though this particular craving wasn't for peaches. He had a terrible yearning to visit someplace whose name started with *B*. Strange how just thinking about a chicken biscuit can brighten an otherwise gloomy day.

"Adam! The fanboy's name is Adam." Sam stomach growled. "But who is he to me?"

Help Wanted

THE project proved entirely impossible to execute on paper. Adam needed to return to the lab, to learn through a series of experiments. After another week of purely theoretical work, he was sure of only one thing: it was impossible to prune a tree so dense with plausible outcomes. He yearned for clean, well-lit surfaces fitted with all the right tools—only then could he subdue these perverse puzzle pieces, hone their shape, force them to fit.

Why had he made such an ambitious proposal in the first place? He should have only committed to prototyping the sustainable alternative meta-energy. Trying to concurrently use that energy to fuel a first-of-a-kind breakthrough was nonsense, pure nonsense. He had set the bar too high. Significant pieces were mostly in place, but the only true scientific advance was a real bust, a boom rather: the releasing of a huge amount of uncontrollable energy.

"Boom! Underline 'uncontrollable' twice."

"Sam, I didn't expect to hear from you now that the money's gone."

"It's not always about the money."

"And only a few pieces work reliably. There must be a way out."

"You know there's a way out."

"Do not."

"Yes, you do, Adam. You just don't want to pitch your invention as a weapon of mass destruction." Adam could never do that. He was sure those who weaponized such technology never slept soundly again—and SAM, SAM would be the worst of the worst, worse than a planet killer, more deadly than an ender of galaxies. A minute with SAM might end all life in all dimensions. "You don't think they've already realized they have a WMD in the making?"

Adam stopped listening. Maybe he would visit the lab to see how the repairs were coming along. His paper exercise would soon be over. He needed to reach the next milestone as soon as possible to trigger another funding installment. His work had to continue, even if he had to cheat to make his dreams come true.

"Don't do it." Of course, Adam wasn't going to do it. So what if he spent the last twenty years of his life working on something that might never be. "Parenting's like that too, bro."

"Sam, don't try to change the subject and never, never call me bro. Parenting is nothing like time travel." It couldn't be. Nothing Sam said made sense, not really. Parenting … and time travel? Adam stopped to consider the possible tie between the two most difficult challenges in his life. "OK, so a parent knows all too well about the risks a child will face—even when that child has no clue."

"Examples?"

"How to cross the street … how to not join the wrong crowd—"

"How to not get pregnant before marriage."

"Sam, you really know how to end a conversation. OK, so the knowledge paradox does make time travel a lot like parenting."

Maybe the worst part is that what we really want for our child, or for ourselves, may never become real.

For Adam, waiting was the hardest of all things. Yes, the lab would be rebuilt, though the source of this money now required frequent updates to monitor the project's safety compliance as well as its actual progress. Once again, there was nothing to report, save another brick in the wall. The external fortifications would soon be in place, allowing the alarm system to be activated—then Adam could finally relax. He secretly added a temporary surveillance camera and gave strict instructions that no one should cross the crime scene tape which quarantined the project's intellectual property.

SAM was all over the floor—well, heaped in a pile on the cold hard floor. Adam's eyes welled with tears. His sanity hinged upon an insignificant fact: he would be gone before the construction paused for lunch. He didn't want to interact with anyone. He didn't even want to think. Could his life's work really be the sum of this huddled mass of broken parts? The longer he breathed in this melancholy, the more profound the droop in his shoulders, the slack in his jaw.

He turned his back to the buzz of construction bees, removing his glasses to wipe his eyes. For a second, he let go of his pain. A rush of possibilities pinged his senses. Was that wonderful smell bread or chocolate chip cookies? He closed his eyes to better sample this fresh-from-the-oven delight. It tasted of honey.

The urgent sweetness reminded him of her lips. Did he have to go so soon? He raised his arms to touch the mist. Was she here, with him, in this moment? He could almost make out her face....

Adam opened his eyes and immediately regretted that mistake.

Something strange caught his attention. He squinted. What was that something in the mist just beyond his reach?

The exit door seemed as two doors without his glasses.

Still his heart ached. He could never look upon her and not see his true love behind that mask.

Which should he pick? The one on the left or the one on the right?

He laughed if only out of misery, as if forever lost in a maze of complexity.

How does one make such an impossible decision without more information, without any additional insight as to what might be waiting behind each of those doors?

He waited for inspiration.

He would go to the right, yes, to the right, ready to face whatever wonders, whatever terrors—

"Hey!" There was only one door now.

Had the unchosen path vanished before his eyes?

"The journal!" Adam ran back to his office to retrieve the project journal. There it was, on his desk, safe and sound.

If she were gone, could he breathe? Would life go on? Might his world simply refuse to spin?

As he turned to leave, he discovered a roll of barrier tape adorning his wrist. It reminded him of the bracelet he wore as a teenager. He sealed the office-closet's entrance with a serious looking *X*.

Who could have predicted how quickly the green would drain out of the planet? He was lucky to have secured passage, though Mars would never have been his first choice. The journey wasn't as bad as it might have been, especially after that asteroid grazed the boat.

He stopped two, nearly three steps from the escape hatch. Three, two, one. He pressed the big red button. A gust of air equalized the pressure in the tunnel between the ship and the rescue shuttle.

"See ya later, Mr. Driver."
Adam leaned into the door with his left shoulder. He didn't say goodbye. He didn't say anything.

The clearing of the neighboring grounds began a week or two after the start of building repairs. Once the largest holes were filled in, the stone and brick were delivered. The arborist put yellow ribbons round the keepers and big red *X*'s on the lost souls. She also marked the stumps as many laborers, even some leaders, seemed eager to ignore any difficult task. If she hadn't, the near field would have been suited for little more than homes for small creatures and oversized flower pots.

"What's this little gem?" The arborist spotted a small box near one of the most damaged trees. The box was in surprisingly good shape and especially heavy for its size. Oddly, a brass plate had been affixed to its side. "Please deliver to Adam Driver." Strange. Well, he did blow a hole in his building and take out all those defenseless trees—why wouldn't he leave his toys lying about? She tried to open the box. It was locked.

"Hello there!"

Wendy looked for the person, or perhaps parrot, who called to her. "Is that you, Polly?"

"No, it's me, Pauly," Pauly answered as she appeared from behind the building. "I have something for your husband." Wendy tried not to laugh as she bit her lip, hoping Pauly wasn't offering crackers. "I found this box addressed to Mr. Driver."

"Thank you … Pauly." Pauly smiled but didn't speak. "I'll take it to Adam after I check on progress in the lab."

"The stumps will come out next week."

"Great. Thanks again, Pauly." Wendy thought she heard a squawk as Pauly disappeared, blending into the yellowing greens of neighboring foliage. "What a woman: part parrot, part chameleon!"

Wendy hardly remembered the status of the lab as she returned home, sometimes giggling uncontrollably, sometimes wondering what it was about Pauly that made her laugh. She never even gave the small green box a second thought; it seemed a trifle compared to the joy of laughter.

"Where's the box?"

"What?"

"Pauly called. I almost hung up at first. Sounded like a prank call."

"Lots of squawking?"

"Yes," Adam laughed, "squawking and flapping. I heard her say 'Polly' over and over again, but it took me nearly two minutes to get the gist of her message."

"Then you realized she was saying 'Pauly'—right?"

"Exactly! Once I knew she wasn't a parrot, the word 'bawks' made much more sense."

"Your 'bawks' is in the trunk."

Adam carried the gem into the kitchen. Without thinking, he unlocked the box using the smallest key on his chain. It took a bit of patience to navigate through the mass of taped bubble wrap.

"A journal?" Adam turned to the bookmarked page. "It's from ten years in the future."

March 15: Traveling backward in time is much harder than expected. Though not ideal, it's unlikely that additional attempts will result in a better outcome.

The book looked—it felt—eerily familiar, much like the one Wendy gave him when they were in college.

"Wen, why did you mark this page?"

"I didn't. The box isn't from me," she hollered from the living room, already on her way to Adam.

"But Wen, isn't this the bookmark you gave me in college?"

Wendy kissed Adam. She beamed with joy. "You kept it all these years!"

Adam felt strangely complete … till the hairs on the back of his neck stood on end. "Can't be."

"What's wrong?"

"It seems like it's from the future, but it isn't."

Wendy took the journal from Adam. She smiled. She recognized it too. "That's your handwriting."

"Yes … and yet, no. I think it's a forgery."

"Right. It's probably a forgery. Someone took your collegiate journal, wrote a fake entry in your handwriting, and buried it next to a tree in a lot where your future time travel laboratory would be built."

"Quite devious indeed … but why the ides of March? Something about settling a debt?"

"What are you talking about?"

"March fifteenth was the historical Roman deadline for settling debts."

"But why pretend it's from the future?"

"A misdirection?" Adam studied the handwriting. "Too much jitter. It's a good forgery, but look there and there—too much jitter in the stroke."

"Maybe you were hungry when you wrote it."

"No, I don't get hungry anymore."

"Huh?"

"I practice preventative eating."

"Preventative?"

"Why not? We apply the same concept to our belongings, finances, even our teeth. Why not include eating? Seems like a logical extension if not a direct corollary to dental care." Wendy didn't interrupt; she didn't want to wreck Adam's train of thought. "Besides insurance, security systems protect our valuables, portfolio diversification our finances. Don't get me started on the importance of flossing."

"And for eating?"

"Ah, yes, mastication as we call it. I eat every ninety minutes while I'm awake and nothing while I sleep."

"I wouldn't have thought to hold off while sleeping."

"You're kidding, right? Anyway, since I interval eat, I never actually get hungry."

"So that's why you've gained forty pounds."

"Nonsense." Adam turned his head and whispered to himself: barely thirty-two.

"So you weren't hungry when you wrote it … maybe sometime over the next ten years your hand will shake a little."

"That makes sense."

"See."

"That's why the future year was referenced! To cover for the handwriting glitches!"

"You're impossible."

"Probably. No, wait. I didn't write this entry."

"Adam, why is it so hard for you to believe that you will eventually invent time travel?"

"I don't make my *r*'s like that." Wendy made a face. "What? You think this is real? That I invent an infinite and stable power source and leverage that power to drive a time travel device? And then, after all that, I find the need to convince my younger self to trust my instincts, to push through all adversity—to risk the multiverse? So that I can what? Tell myself to eat less, floss better?"

"Has anyone told you lately that you're impossible? You haven't even read the rest of the entry. Maybe it tells you not to build a doomsday device."

"That's impossible. How could my future self tell me not to do the very thing that gave him/me the opportunity to write and deliver the note? If I stop now, the note doesn't get written. If the note isn't written, I would never consider stopping."

"Let's assume you're right—"

"Obviously."

Wendy frowned. Her eyes grew so very sharp, so very pointy. "So, let's assume you're right. There is no paradox. Why would you, or anyone pretending to be you, not want you to push that little red button?"

Adam wasn't listening. A hand-drawn design document had fallen out of the journal.

Wendy and Adam were in bed, together yet separate, one absorbed in computer games, the other busy catching up with internet friends. After nearly twenty minutes, Wendy interrupted the silence.

"I worry about our son not finding true love."

"Huh?" Adam pulled out an earbud. "Were you talking to me?"

"I said I worry our son won't find his true love."

"He will, Wendy. It's just a matter of time."

"How can you be sure?"

"He's a lot like me."

Wendy wrapped her arms around Adam. He hesitated. Maybe she misunderstood. He meant some people struggle a lifetime to fulfill a dream, that he'd like to see his son accomplish something really big. What did she think he said?

"Anyway," Adam mused, "failure is learning."

"Did you just change the subject? Can't you read my mind?"

"I hope—"

"I'm losing hope … and that certain feeling."

"Self-deception is a common form of hope."

Wendy turned over and bit her lip. "Hope just died."

How could hope die? The world is full of it.

Adam couldn't sleep. He kept thinking how other technology leaders had assistants. He'd be a better man and seek that help. Tomorrow.

Why not tonight?

Tomorrow.

Why not tonight?

OK! Adam searched for job sites. He cut and pasted a vague description into a form and hit enter. Was asking for help the same as failing? He always tried his best to fail fast.

He smiled. He might be way ahead of schedule now, having failed so quickly.

Wait. If failure is learning, and asking for help is failure, then wouldn't the least independent, the least capable students make the most progress? Well, they might make the most relative forward progress but they won't get the best grades. Those who already know what they're doing get the best—

Oh. So our education system teaches only the disadvantaged? Then rewards them with mediocre grades? How can they find work with those GPAs? If they can't work in their field, they'll have to settle for lousy dead-end jobs. Low pay … a mountain of debt. "Welcome to the new millennium."

"Go to sleep, Adam."

Wendy turned off her light.

The Lure of Black Leather

AT twenty-six, Addison was all grown up. When she entered a room all eyes lingered on her brow, studied the glow of her cheeks, craved to trace the curve of her lips. A goddess among mortals, only she could warm the sun.

Hundreds of hands were ready to catch her, but she chose to walk alone on the highest of tightropes. She would never accept an easy life. She even refused—deferred as the family attorney put it—her trust money. She needed no net. She wanted no net, not since … not since her mother passed.

No, she preferred to work part time in retail or as a waitress. She had interviewed for a couple of other jobs in offices, large offices with far too many eyes. She wanted more of a family atmosphere, someplace that attracted children too young to date.

She rarely stayed long in any particular position, moving on when things got too heated, when her tips grew too outrageous. Only once did her boss ask her to leave. It was her most recent job; it lasted only two weeks. People started lining up for the blue plate special. The owner was thrilled at first, till he learned Addison's tips exceeded his profit by a factor of ten. The difference was really twenty fold but she tried to save his dignity.

She enjoyed the first few days of freedom, spent some time in the city, did a lot of reading. When she started to do some serious self-reflection, she knew she needed a change. She was world-weary, worn-out, tired of being so damn pretty. Sure, she could live off her beauty alone. A model's life was glamorous—but she didn't want glamor; she despised glamor. She hated how all manner of ties and blouses were loosened when a glamorous person stepped onto the red carpet. The air boiled with infatuation.

Yes, her beauty was a detriment: she confused men, well, mostly men. She distracted them and made them act as children who craved their next sugar fix. But she wasn't candy; she wasn't even sweet. If a person could ignore her looks for five minutes, he or she might find a worthy opponent, a worthy companion, maybe both.

She would dress blandly, awkwardly, if that were possible. It would be cheaper and certainly minimize the hopeless staring. Her life would be better if she acted out of touch, outside the pulse of things. She could pretend to be ignorant of fashion, unaware of good taste. All materials were trendy, any color matched any and all other colors, right? She would fill her closet full of over-sized tops and loose-fitting jeans.

Even if her wardrobe budget could be padded for a few months, she still needed to eat. She was tired of ramen noodles and stretching leftovers. She needed a better paying job—then she could buy all sorts of non-designer clothing, maybe even move into a boxy apartment.

She read for over an hour but couldn't fall asleep. She checked for new job postings. Wow! She hadn't expected to find one this good so quickly—and it was just posted. Tomorrow will be great.

"Oh, crap, what am I going to wear?"

When Addison arrived, she found Wendy at the break table sipping a cup of coffee, fiddling with something in her lab coat pocket. Addison cleared her throat. "I'm here to interview for your opening."

"Oh, right, Adam's new posting. I expect him about nine. Do you mind waiting?"

"No problem. Thank you." Addison smiled. She would be the first to interview.

"Help yourself to tea or—"

The lab door swung open. Adam entered with an odd ferocity, tossing his jacket toward the coat rack without looking. He missed by more than a foot. He pointed firmly and shouted, "Stay!"

Addison laughed. Today, she would laugh at everything.

She followed him into a tiny office, filled with stacks of books, piles of papers. Adam offered her a seat, then stuck his head outside the office, calling out to no one in particular: "If you see Sam, send him in."

"Sam?" Addison's eyes brightened. "Who's Sam?"

"A trusted confidant," Adam answered as he took his seat, pushing aside a stack of books to get a clear view of his redheaded candidate. He knew his description of Sam was too vague. He hadn't intended to make Sam sound mysterious—no, that would have been a mistake. But how could he even attempt to give a more accurate response? Wouldn't she be even more disconcerted if he said his giving an accurate answer depended upon some uncertain facts? Yes, facts are usually facts, but he didn't want to scare her off by sharing too much, especially anything that made him seem a madman.

Addison smiled throughout the awkward silence, waiting for the interview to start.

Truthfully, Adam felt uneasy about allowing himself to make any assumptions about the nature of time. Time had a way of masking changes or rewriting history so as to make someone or something more or less important in the overall scheme of things. Was time still linear? Was Sam alive in this dimension?

Addison could see the pain on Adam's face.

He didn't even know if this was a 'Before Sam' or 'After Sam' moment. Should he laugh or cry, not knowing what was real, what had been or was yet to be?

"What timeline is this?" The words were out and circled the room before Adam realized he had shifted from thinking to talking.

"Sorry, I didn't quite understand your question. But if you were referring to time travel, I believe the real question is how to generate enough energy."

Adam's eyes lit up. "The energy requirement doesn't need to be met in a single step. Look closely." Adam reached into his pocket and placed his pride and joy on the desk with a thud.

"It's so small."

Adam frowned. Size did matter. "'Mighty oaks from little acorns grow.' A. B. Johnson."

Addison laughed. Johnson, good one. "*The Philosophical Emperor a Political Experiment*, 1841. I prefer Chaucer's 'As an ook cometh of a litel spyr.'"

"*Troilus and Criseyde*, 1374," Adam added for completeness.

Addison smiled. She was impressed.

Adam closed his eyes to gather his thoughts. She was a kind of kindred spirit, wasn't she?

"Anyway," Adam continued, "each press of the button doubles the energy, ignoring dampening effects. The design was modeled after the audial decibel law where volume doubles with every increase of 10 dB. It's usually better to model something after a principle in nature rather than make up the rules as you go."

"So the initial energy level is determined by a seed mass?" Addison hypothesized as much as asked.

"Yes, by the seed mass. After the first button push, the volume— um, the mass—is altered in ten increments until the energy stabilizes at double the initial level. Each increment is analyzed to determine if it is sufficient to trigger system activation. If not, the process continues until all ten increments are evaluated."

"If more energy is required, can the button be pressed again?"

"Yes! The energy output doubles each time the mass is divided by the next fraction in a sequence defined by one divided by two to the nth power, where n is a positive integer: one-half, one-quarter, one-eighth, and so on."

"As the fraction shrinks, won't the energy continue to increase all the way to infinity?"

"Yes, this divide-by-zero technology offers that possibility, but in practice the increased energy would either become sufficient to trigger system activation or blow up the lab."

Addison laughed.

Wow, she was beautiful, intelligent—and fearless. Adam paused to catch his breath.

"Addy, can I call you Addy?" She nodded. "Addy, here's the big picture. The energy could be available for all stages, but it's currently only used for stage three. First stage, Select, defines the destination. For testing, we've hardcoded that destination to be 'yesterday on Table *B*.' The second stage, Acquire, requires the system to locate the selected destination through a complex algorithm that validates key events. And finally, stage three, Map, transfers the object to the specified destination. Of course, the Map stage must first capture the to-be-transferred object through digital encapsulation … that source object, again for simplicity, is assumed to be on Table *A*. Once the Map stage has completed the encapsulation, the object is converted from its digital representation to an analog matter-based copy at the selected destination and voilà!"

Sam had arrived about the same time as Adam but preferred to ease into the day. He could, in fact, sleep through lunch on days when the air was rife with acronyms. Science wasn't his strong suit. He didn't have the patience for all the conjectures and especially shied from any and all consequences. He preferred math—or 'maths' as he might say to someone he suspected of loving British accents. Statistics were in his wheelhouse. Facts were real; people were unpredictable and overly concerned with silly things like money, power, and cat videos.

An uncontrollable grin enveloped Sam's face. "Wow, she is stunning."

He gasped. What if she caught him gawking? He cast his eyes to the far corner of the room.

His pulse raced as he imagined her body wrapped in black leather.

"Well, almost voilà," she said, "there are some small details about how to bend the selected timeline."

"You're hired. See you tomorrow, nine a.m."

"Thank you, Dr. Driver." She offered her hand.

His heart skipped a beat. He needed to steady himself. An odd weave of fear and delight blotched his face. Her hand was strong yet soft enough for galaxies to war for her touch.

Before he could breathe, she was gone. Only her perfume remained.

Shhhhikt!

The walls began to slide closer and closer, clicking louder and louder, knocking down pile after pile of books.

His foot was trapped. He tugged and tugged, leaping through the doorway at the last possible second.

Wendy greeted him outside the office. "So, what do you think?"

"Beautiful."

"Yes, I can see she made an impression on you."

"What? No … oh, right. We're all set."

"'Cause she interviewed so beautifully? Did you tell her you're not a doctor of anything?"

"Yes, I've hired someone. Tell everyone else our position has been filled."

"Why are you wearing only one shoe?"

"I have to run out for some, ah, parts; might take the rest of the day."

Adam perched high on a ladder to reinforce SAM's ventilation mechanism, which looked very much like a straw with a pinstripe running its length. Sam had a way of making subtle useless changes—useless from a functional point of view. Sam's approximation of pop art wasn't lost on Adam.

"How about burgers for lunch?" Wendy didn't answer. She had been bracing the ladder. Why was she turned round, waving her hands so wildly?

"Adam, here she comes!" Adam noticed the end of the chassis didn't quite line up with the rest of the stripe. He must have severed the band when he adjusted the angle of inclination. "Adam!"

"Wen, I need to focus."

"Did you see her look down as she entered the lab? Something's bothering that girl."

"Wen, I'm working—unless you want to climb up here."

Adam didn't see the anger spread from her knitted brow, through her piercing eyes, to the center of her gaping mouth. Uh-oh, she's biting her upper lip—

"Adam," she whispered. "Adam!" she screamed. He would pay to supersized her double cheeseburger and for so much more. Why was he so callous toward the women in his life?

"Addy has more than enough work queued for today. She'll be fine."

"You can't just throw a myriad of unrelated tasks at her. She needs perspective."

"Tell her to retrieve the relevant book when she begins a new task."

"I'm not going to tell her to retrieve anything. She isn't a dog. You tell her."

"Seriously? You want me to stop fixing this key structural element, climb all the way down this ladder just to tell her she isn't a dog?"

Wendy didn't respond. Something was wrong, something was very wrong. Don't look down. Don't look down.

Adam looked down. Wendy returned a glare that spoke volumes. He knew not to argue with that particular contortion … that face could break glass. He'd have to fix his spider sense and probably his watch.

Since when was Wendy so protective? Shouldn't two alpha women hate each other?

"So it has come to this."

"I heard that. Be ready to leave in ninety minutes. I'm getting the fish and the double burger, both supersized. You're drinking water until you get that 'minus ten' working."

"I finished that yesterday."

"Then run it again. You're getting fat."

There used to be a twinkle in her eyes when she said things like that. What had turned her against him? She used to love being interrupted in the kitchen. Now she always has a knife in her hand.

Adam called sheepishly to Addy. She didn't hear him. She was listening to music. Adam touched her shoulder to get her attention. Their eyes met and locked hard. Adam tried to look away but couldn't; their connection was too strong. Both began to sway as if they were dancing. Addy stirred her hips.

"Come in my office whenever you want. I mean, please come … into my office … when you need … information, yes, background information for your tasks. My shelves are busting … er … bursting? … bursting with…." Addy looked confused. Adam continued helplessly. "You can come … even if I'm not there."

Adam turned and hurried toward his office. He stopped abruptly. She might follow … too many eyes … certainly not enough time. He walked out of the lab. He would wait in the car for ninety minutes. He had done that a thousand times. He could do it again.

Wendy offered several alternatives to advance the project at a more controlled pace, but she wasn't sure Adam was listening. He didn't give any feedback. He didn't even make eye contact. Wendy dangled a french fry in front of his face.

"Great, now that I have your attention, I think we should scale back the next steps. We don't need to move mountains. Less mass means less risk."

Adam agreed but said nothing. He had already decided to use a pre-encapsulated source object and a small one at that ... maybe a grape. Green? Red? Black? Did it really matter? Green. Seeded or seedless? Damn it, seedless. Why was science so demanding?

"And you should tell Addy about Sam."

"I'm going to walk home," Adam declared as he finished his sandwich. He needed to avoid all the conversations, all the beauty at work.

Wendy was visibly upset as she drove back to the lab. She resented being stuck behind the curtain. She needed to be a full partner. And why was he so invested in the current design? He rejected every new idea. She couldn't change his mind on anything. He was the most stubborn—

She shook her head. She couldn't change him. She couldn't even change herself.

As Wendy completed reconfiguring the field stability parameters, she began the validation step. It was too easy to flip the wrong bit. Why did Adam build this next generation technology out of antiquated parts? DIP switches, really? Sometimes, he was so binary.

"What's up, Ms. Wendy?"

"Addy, you startled me." Wendy blushed as she hid the long, thin rod behind her back. "I was thinking about work, about Adam and wishing."

"Wishing?"

"And wondering ... wondering why he says what he says. Last night he told me, 'A man needs more than one black tea in his life.'"

"Is that code for something?"

"I wish. He was lamenting how we have no English Breakfast in the cupboard." Wendy shook her head. "Men are such simple creatures. All they need is food, drink, and a little success at work."

"I think you forgot at least one thing on that list."

"Sleep?"

Addy laughed. "What were you really doing when I walked in? Were you trying to make Adam's thingy go? Were you flipping his switches?"

"Adam is a man."

"Say no more. He won't stop for directions, much less let anyone solve his problems."

"He wants us to contribute, but he has to be the one who fits the last piece into the puzzle, the one who makes the breakthrough."

"He wants to be the one who invents time travel."

"He has to be the one who throws the switch or he'll never be whole."

"And when a man's ego droops, so does his—"

"Ms. Addy, don't you dare, don't you dare make me come after you with this pointy stick!"

Adam tried to include Addy in the project, but she didn't have the right skills. She could repeat specific tasks, but didn't have enough experience to improvise new solutions. Adam explained the novel concepts he inserted into the project and even shared stories, now and again, about those who inspired him.

Today's to-do was a simple one, a tweak to the fraction decay rate for the divide-by-zero technology, the big red button as Sam called it. The adjustment had four steps: release the safety, remove the back panel, reduce the decay rate by one, reassemble.

"There are four steps. All begin with *R*." Addy laughed. "Pass me the crescent wrench." Addy passed the crescent wrench. "Pass me the Phillips screwdriver." Addy passed the slot head. "Not the flat one, the one with the cross head." Addy passed the Phillips-headed screwdriver. The decay rate switch was exposed, the one on the right. "What does the DIP say?"

Addy laughed.

He didn't quite understand why she laughed at him, at almost everything he said. It was quite unexpected, quite unusual for a student to giggle at all manner of teachings. To his knowledge, there was nothing inherently humorous about DIP switches, nothing remotely funny about quantum mechanics. It seemed wholly inappropriate and yet somehow quite inventive to joke about such things. It made science seem more real, something you could reach out and touch. Addy made the whole seem greater than the sum of her parts, er, the sum of the parts.

"Addy, the DIP says what?"

Addy laughed.

"What?"

Addy laughed.

"Addy! It's binary: up is one, down is zero. What's the reading?"

"08 in hexadecimal. I prefer hex over binary."

She prefers hex. "And you probably think quarks are something to chew on."

Addy didn't laugh. She made a face. OK, maybe that last part about quarks was a bit too jumbled. Still, it pained him how she made that same face whenever he spoke passionately about power equations. It bothered him how her lips grew more and more confused whenever he quoted his heroes. It was never wrong to praise another's passion … quote their principles, write their equations on the blackest of boards with the thickest of chalks.

"Sorry if that last comment about quarks was too negative."

Addy laughed.

No, they didn't quite speak the same language—oh, yes, the same language but a distinctly different dialect. Each had words and gestures foreign to the other. He had no idea what she meant when she asked about his risking life to create life. He had not even thought of creating life for some years. His work was about recreating. He was sure he had said something about recreating life. Why was she playing with her hair?

"Pass me the pointy thing." Addy laughed as she passed the pointy thing.

Still there was something about her. Her eyes spoke volumes. He understood her eyes. She was asking much better questions now. She seemed interested in the work. She had a certain aptitude for it. As her teacher he must test her knowledge.

"And what's eight hexadecimal minus one?" Again that look—

"Ah, seven?"

"Yes, Addy, seven. So how do we turn our eight into a seven."

"One down, least significant three up."

"And which one goes down?"

"The only one that's up."

The more he thought about it, the more he liked, loved the curves of her smile. He loved all her curves.

He quickly positioned the lab journal just so. His bits were also up.

He tried to maintain a professional relationship but struggled. Sometimes it was his fault; other times she was the one whose eyes locked on him in some intimate way. Was it a crime how easily he connected with her? How her eyes followed him? He hadn't encouraged it as far as he knew. Maybe working so closely forged some unspoken bond. Maybe something about him excited her. Maybe she needed him, wanted him.

It wasn't a crime if she wanted him.

She would probably deny it at first, try to hide from it. She came here for money, not love. Adam smiled at her. She probably looked up to him, admired him, his experience, his knowledge. He could quote axioms with the best of them. Of course, she was the yearning student. She could not yet formulate her work as an operator on a Hilbert space.

And he? He gladly embraced his role as the more mature, more established one, being so close to giving life to his masterpiece. Fate brought them together. She needed exactly what he could offer—no, not just a job. Work was the last thing on his mind. Honestly, he didn't care that much about the stupid project anymore. He was tired. Tired of pushing that impossible string. He needed a break, a distraction from grinding out an impossible career. Publish or perish—he was sick of it, year after year: perish, perish, perish. His creations were pieces, not papers. He couldn't divulge those pieces without betraying the puzzle. He wanted more from life ... to be more, see more, do more. Love roots quickly and knows no bounds in such fertile ground. He tickled her with his eyes. He felt dirty—dirty and curious. Off with that sweater, that top, those pants. He needed a long drink from this fountain.

Addy smiled. She knew what he was thinking.

Adam smiled back. He had been falling for such a long time and she caught him. She caught him. Addy asked a question, but Adam didn't understand. He was grinning like a school boy. He should have felt embarrassed, but he didn't. School boys don't know enough about real life to get embarrassed.

She smiled again. Maybe she felt warm and safe, knowing they would soon be together. Maybe she wanted it more with each passing second.

Why hadn't he kissed her yet? His pulse raced. He tried to calm himself as he did years ago before a competition … but he wasn't on the track. He wasn't in high school. He was middle-aged, married with children, two mostly grown children.

How could he? He was mud. He hated sitting in this puddle. He needed this something, this someone to help him up.

He reached for her hand. She was warm, soft. He couldn't let go.

He wanted her everything.

Luck

We are what we believe we are.
–C. S. Lewis

Rolled-up aces. Keep a straight face. Take control before someone with a middle pair hits a set on the flop.

Two Few Outs

"RAISE!"

Sam wouldn't shut up. He couldn't. Women love bad boys.

"Pocket rockets?"

"Yep, pocket rockets."

Adam shook his head. "We need to run diagnostics and double check the support frame." Surely she knew aces hit a player every 221 hands.

"The flop was ugly. A big bet would have chased everyone away."

Adam reached for a wrench, the heaviest in his little red toolbox. So what if the rainbow flop made him a big favorite. Anything can happen on the turn.

"And the turn?" Her eyes softened as if watching her first-ever sunrise.

"A blank. Even important stuff can turn out to be nothing."

Sam had it all but locked down, favored nineteen to one with only one card to come. Only one of the remaining two nines could bust him. She bounced up and down, eager to hear the final card.

"The nine of clubs."

Disappointment spilled from her eyes. Sam lost to a set of nines.

"My aces drowned in the river!"

Laughter.

He would gladly lose a thousand times just to hear her—

"Sam, I could use your help."

"Nonsense, Adam, you played for years."

"He plays too?"

"Ancient history. His clothes aren't the only thing that's a bit too tight."

Sam's next hole cards were A-K suited. He wanted action.

An older clean-shaven guy in middle position bet fifteen. He could have anything—if he wasn't super tight. He had a big pair, but how big? The only way to find out was to re-raise.

"Re-raise." Sam pushed in fifty. The pot was now sixty-eight, no, sixty-four. The dealer just took the rake.

Would the old guy call or raise? If he called, he probably had queens or jacks. A re-raise put him on aces or kings.

"Re-raise." The old guy fumbled chips as he counted out two hundred. Sam could go all-in but the old guy would call any raise. No bluff could win Sam the hand.

"Call."

The flop· A-,J-10, one heart, two diamonds.

"Check." The old guy checked? Oh, he has K-K, not A-A. How much can Sam bet and keep this fish on the hook?

"Two hundred." Even if the guy thought Sam had an ace, he'd be getting sufficient odds to draw for trips or the flush.

He's taking his time.

Sam knew what the old guy was thinking. He doesn't like putting more money into a pot where he might be behind. Sam looked him right in the eye.

"All-in."

What? The old guy went all-in?

And he's smiling!

Sam replayed the hand in his mind. Re-raising pre-flop implied Sam had a big hand like A-A, K-K, A-K, Q-Q, or J-J. When the ace hit, a bet on the flop narrowed Sam's cards to A-A, A-K, or J-J. Then Sam looked the old guy straight in the eye—

Shit! Showing strength meant weakness. Sam all but shouted he was holding A-K.

Wait. The old guy had a pair of kings. Sam had aces. Why would the old guy go all-in when he's a dog? How much money was that bet?

"How much is it?" The dealer counted the old dog's all-in bet: two-fifty-five, no, two-fifty-six. The old dog had a dollar chip protecting his cards. So he bet $256 rather than call $200. Makes sense. If he had just called, his last fifty-six would have gone in at

some point. No one would surrender a monster for a mere fifty bucks.

Adam stepped into his office to escape Sam's story. He knew such tales inside and out having lived in that world for a year's worth of weekends. The walls seemed so close. The room was a cage, a breeding ground for claustrophobia.

Adam started to whistle.

Was it Tuesday or Wednesday? The days ran together, each one pretending to be another.

He peered through a small portion of clear glass, a peep hole of sorts. Only the name tag was transparent; the rest of the door was scalloped within an inch of its life. The room needed a focal point, somewhere to look besides the cluttered desk.

Why was the filing cabinet open? Adam never used that contraption. He rejected that his life could be boiled down to some alphabetical order. He preferred to stack his papers so that each pile meant something.

"What's in that pile, the second from the right?"

Sam called the all-in bet and showed his hand. The old dog half-beamed, half-sneered as he turned over his pocket kings. The old dog mumbled he had no choice; he was pot committed.

The turn was a king. The lucky dog hit a set.

"You had two pair. He had three kings," Adam shouted from his office.

"That's what I said." Sam stared at Adam before continuing.

The lucky dog stood up. He seemed oddly happy as if his blood was flowing for the first time in a decade, maybe two. He started rooting for a deuce, any deuce, any deuce but the deuce of diamonds. He wanted a blank on the river, not a flush.

"Queen," the dealer called out. There was a bit of surprise in her voice. Had she too been rooting for a two?

"So you guys split?"

"Hell no! The queen was a diamond. I hit the straight flush!"

"So you both didn't have the straight? You won with the royal flush?"

"Adam! You know the ranking of poker hands."

"Did the dealer say 'queen' or 'queen of diamonds'?"

"Why does it matter? The royal flush is a once-in-a-lifetime hand."

"Then give her the respect she deserves. Put a diamond on it."

Six months earlier …

The fading light forced Adam to squint. He could barely make out the canvas, much less understand why the giddy Parisian blue chased the buttery red across the sky.

His chest ached. His brush dropped dead on the palette.

He wasn't having a heart attack. He recognized this pain as something much more dangerous. Everything would be so much easier if he hadn't looked into her eyes.

Time vanished as Addy pulled the last blind shut. Adam seemed anxious as he maneuvered into position.

"A little higher. You'll never get it from there."

Adam held tightly with both hands before repositioning his feet.

She was right. He could reach everything from here.

"Adam?"

He smiled. It was tighter than expected.

"Adam, I can't. I just can't."

Adam knew she was speaking but didn't hear her words. "Almost there," he offered as a plausible response.

Addy bit her lower lip. She would count down from one hundred. Ninety-nine.

"Done!"

"I know. I could tell."

Adam started down the ladder. The new fasteners snuggly held the flute to the support frame.

"Ready?"

"Adam, I can't."

"You can't what?"

"I can't do this anymore."

"Nonsense, it can be an everyday thing now that the tubing is secure."

"No."

"Look, it's easy. When I point at you, you push the button."

Adam hoisted himself onto the oversized white table and pointed at Addy.

Addy stood motionless. No meant no.

"The little red one." How did a button of such immense importance get such a belittling name? Adam looked at Addy, then again at his button. It wasn't all that little, not really.

Adam double-checked the stack of clothes. Good. He had remembered the belt.

"Addy, the little red one if you please."

Addy shook her head. "We didn't test all the changes."

"Addy, just push it."

"I can't." She wasn't going to push or pull anything.

"I understand."

Adam did not understand. He dropped from Table *A* and stomped his way to the control panel. He wouldn't ask a fifth time for anything. He wanted Sam to remember the last two years, but the old cloned image would have to do.

Adam pressed the little red button.

Addy closed her eyes. If the world was about to end, she didn't want—

"Addy! Watch that gauge! I have to adjust the overflow valve!"

"What's happening?"

"We're spewing too much juice!"

The high-pitched whistle dropped an octave before Adam reached the top of the ladder. The trial was over before it began. A lifetime of sweat and toil—and still no Sam on Table *B*.

The flute wasn't even in tune.

Adam looked pale as Addy pulled him from the floor.

"What happened?"

"You fainted."

Adam squeezed her hand.

"You can let go now."

"I'm surprised I didn't break anything."

"You were only one step up when you fell."

"The flute failed?"

"You forgot the condom."

Adam looked away. "I meant to bring one."

Addy bit her lip. "We need to rethink the release valve."

Adam sighed. He hated change. So much could go wrong. If he hadn't found that design document, he would have abandoned the flute concept months ago. It wasn't a question of whether this or that button was big or not. The flute had once controlled the energy flow; it would again.

Adam waited ages for this moment. Was she ready?

"Now, Adam? Should I push?"

Adam's eyes grew big. He could barely move his lips. He blinked as if counting down from ten.

"Now? The little red one?"

"Big." Adam cleared his throat. "The big one."

"I don't see any—"

"Look again." Adam winked at SAM.

"Oh." Her finger circled the edge of his big red button. Adam blushed. Her finger kept circling and circling—

"Just push the damn thing."

Addy pushed hard on the big red button. SAM rattled louder and louder as larger and larger pebbles flowed through his pipes.

"What's happening?"

Adam didn't answer. His eyes were locked on the ripple forming four feet off the lab floor. Was it alive? Bursts of light … hypnotic … such perfect violets, such perfect blues—

"Adam!" Addy cried out as a bolt of lightning shot through the ceiling.

"Sam?" Adam pleaded. "Are you there?"

The metallic hulk clinked in bings and bangs as the rift flickered in and out. Rows of LEDs sputtered. A falling ceiling tile bounced off Adam's glove hand.

Adam lowered his head. "Right field all over again."

"Adam, you're not making any sense. Adam!" Her panic spilled onto the floor. She had to do something, anything. She jerked erratically as if combining ballet with jujitsu. The lights flickered an impromptu accompaniment.

Adam was oblivious, still captivated by the void where his baby once danced.

"Adam?"

"Yes, Addy." There was something devious in his smile as he picked up the pointy thing.

"So, your project—"

"Our project."

"So, our project connects an infinite power source to an experimental machine?"

Adam didn't answer.

"Adam, please answer my question."

"Sorry, I didn't hear it as a question."

"And?"

"Yes, Addy, you are correct, but can we talk about—"

"Did you consider all the what-ifs?"

"Every what-if?" Adam looked confused. "Like what-if we vibrate the wrong timeline and every fourth Karl explodes?"

"What-if every time we hit that big red button, we destroy a world?"

"It's unlikely."

"Adam!"

"What-if wearing blue impacts the integrity of the stage two laser? Maybe we should get naked to avoid reflecting blue light." Adam started unbuttoning his shirt.

"What are you doing?"

"Addressing a key what-if."

"Stop undressing your what-if."

"Is that a red light?"

"What-if we snap a timeline?"

"Oh, that's a good one. Sam and I discussed that scenario."

Addy's eyes screamed for an answer.

"Yes, snapping a timeline would be a very bad thing. So we test for activation at every increment, limiting the total energy to 2x for each button push."

"What-if a bug prevents activation? We all die?"

"Yes and no."

Addy bit her lip.

"Look, we cheat death every day."

Addy punched his shoulder.

"Ow! Addy, I get it. You're eager to hear my answer, so let me speak." Adam held Addy's wrists. "I don't like to eat right after I get up, but I do, usually a bowl of cereal and a cup of lemongrass tea. I'd tell you why lemongrass, but I don't want you to hit me again."

"You're not making any sense."

"We have to rely on a fail-safe response."

"Which is?"

"Someone will go back in time and correct our mistakes."

"Seriously, that's your plan: *ixnay* on the *ixfay*? Maybe I should stop you from pushing that damn red button!"

"Wow, I just realized something really cool."

"What? How to survive the Kobayashi Maru?"

"No! And stop encouraging me to cheat." Adam smiled. "Pig latin for OK is okay."

Addy waited for Adam to leave. His office smelled like an old bookstore. Everything seemed to be in chaos. She could see no grouping by subject or project phase or any other organization— except for one book, the log book, which rested squarely on a small side table abutting the far side of the desk. The project log was the only thing on that table, save for pen and pencil.

Addy opened the log book and smiled. Many of the entries seemed to have been first entered in pencil, then traced with pen after a number of corrections. Most of the initial concepts were quite simple but, as she turned the pages, she noticed more and more complex topics being addressed in greater detail. Adam was making progress after all. She could see that now.

But why was he chasing energy generation so aggressively? He could work out all the backend steps with the available power. Humans haven't been able to steer the energy produced by mixing candy with cola. How could he ever realize this dream?

"This drawing shows an infinite energy source being contained by a black hole! Insanity!"

She turned the page. Utter disbelief strangled her face.

"The '!Adam.specific' modification is key as it will screen out those characteristics unique to Adam."

Some godlike shit was happening in this lab. Genetic manipulation, selective cloning? Addy placed the log book back on the side table. She wished she could go back in time and warn herself not to touch that book. There wasn't enough vodka in this town to drink her way out of this discovery.

She now understood what Adam had revealed during her interview. She had been busy trying to impress him with her internet findings, so she never thought to parse out his intent. What did he say? He phrased it as a question, an odd question. "Is it better to divide by zero than live in obscurity?" Seemed innocent at first, but he'd have to break many fundamental laws governing math and physics. He would be risking everything … for what? Fanfare?

Midlife's the B-word

ADAM'S life now flowed as a long and lonely river. It spun round rounder and rounder rocks, occasionally carving new paths through fresh mud. It would be another cold night. Adam's heart stirred as he pulled the covers over his shoulders.

Two hats on the nightstand caught his eye. One was navy with stripes of yellow and white. The other was an odd blend, impersonating some sort of mauvish hue. He studied both toques. The yellow in the first hat bothered him as an unnecessary extravagance. But that second one, in that particular shade of purple, seemed impure, tainted. It could not have been brought to life by a true dyer of the fountain. Such false hope, stained by some cruel carpet weaver, must be rooted out, thrown to the—

Adam gently lifted the nearly violet beanie, kissing it once before tossing it in a velvet arc toward Wendy. The cap landed on the top of a heap of some four dozen such beanies. Adam waited uneasily for a response to cap-request number forty-nine. He hadn't meant for the misunderstood purple beanie to land on the island of dead hats. Wendy had built that island from the ground up. She had crocheted those caps for charity, which naturally Adam took to mean those hats were his to use for this singular purpose.

Winter would soon be upon them. Wendy would then be guarded by any number of buttons and snaps. She'd even tuck the outer edges of the blankets under her body to stay warm—safe and warm. So in June, when Adam accepted the stash of toques as his birthday gift, he knew those fifty opportunities for frivolity had to be exhausted before the first snowfall.

He had missed this deadline, of course, as inventing such things as infinite power is not the least bit possible for a man or woman who cannot suppress everyday thoughts of their partner's affection. Adam's project would have floundered even more miserably though if he hadn't thought to adjust the automatic thermostat to give him an extra hour before his bride wrapped herself as tightly as an Egyptian princess.

She hadn't picked up the cap, hadn't tossed it back to him.

Surely Wendy knew that story, the one about the couple who slept in separate beds. The husband took his cap from the bedpost each night and tossed it to his wife. Who wrote that book? Was it a book? A short story? A folktale passed down from generation to generation to make marriage seem like a reasonable thing to do? The woman had a decision to make: toss the hat or bring the hat back to her partner.

Adam smiled at the thought of adding the story to the lab journal where Wendy would find it waiting for her. She would return beanie number fifty. He was sure she would.

The last of the day's sadness wandered to the farthest corner of the bedroom, twirled once, twice, before dropping heavily onto a bed of carpet fuzz.

"Tell me you didn't fail another spelling test. She must have been furious."
"She doesn't know."
"She doesn't know, yet."
"Don't threaten me or I'll—"
"Adam?"
"Yes, Mom."
"Who were you talking to?"

Adam pawed at the snooze button before retreating under heavy layers of bedding. The day could start without him. He would enjoy his morning as a bump in a bed.

The alarm rang again. His turtle head peeked from its blanket-shell. He pulled his pillow to his chest. He hadn't been to the lab for a week. What was one more day?

Adam reached for a pencil. He appreciated the feel of a good number two between his thumb and forefinger.

His hand stopped mid scribble. He could hear a faint yet crisp tapping, likely made by a small foot in a high quality shoe. But he dared not look up. He could not. These maths would not solve themselves.

The alarm rang again.

How could he complete such an impossible equation with all these interruptions? This page would simply not yield to his stare, not reveal its formula's true purpose. Could it be a lookahead algorithm to trigger the kill switch?

A horrific shadow obscured his view. He waved his hands but the blotch stood its ground. What was the source of all this—

"Hello?"

Oh, a woman, someone of great import by the fit of her attire, the sound of her footwear. Was she wanting him?

The alarm rang again.

A blur of red rushed past him. His world pinched and stretched, pulling thinner and thinner. Through the key hole went his desk, his books, his number two pencil. He was alone in an overly warm room.

The alarm! Adam kicked off the covers.

"What time is it?" He glanced at the clock then sprang from bed, pulling on his jeans, grabbing his backpack before running down the stairs. He pushed hard against the exit door to get it to budge, even harder to force the gap wide enough to squeeze out.

A cold breeze surprised him. It must be fall, late fall.

He had been here before. The buildings were familiar, though unusually pristine. Perhaps the rain....
Something was out of place. Maybe many things were out of place. This quad shouldn't be here. It lives in east campus, not south.

"Am I nineteen or thirty-nine?"

If he didn't hurry, he would miss the final. He could run. If he were nineteen, he'd get there with just enough time to rush through the exam. Get where exactly? He searched his pockets, his pack. Maybe the schedule was in his desk. He rummaged through his dorm room, his office, but found nothing.

How could he ever find anything with all this clanging? Chuck would know.

Adam saw his roommate reading at his desk.
"Chuck?" Nothing. "Chuck?" Chuck began to fade.

Grief overwhelmed Adam. He should have hugged him before it was too late. The alarm rang and rang. It wouldn't stop ringing.

Adam sat up without even considering putting one foot out of bed. He knew this day would come. Yet somehow anticipating its arrival only hurried it along. He was neither tired nor motivated and especially had no desire whatsoever to repeat the mundane tasks which stalked this and every morning. How could taking a shower or brushing his teeth make a difference? How could eating breakfast or walking to work uncover the elusive secret which kept his dream just out of reach?

More than he realized, his inspiration took wing from the little things of life: the typical and trivial, like how the temperatures were now sliding into winter. He would normally linger to absorb such sugar-moments, but not today. He didn't even think to search for the one or two cold spots on his pillow.

He looked down at his hands and frowned: the dark spots would soon win the day. When did his right hand get so thick, his fingers so stubby? He absentmindedly reached up and rubbed the bald spot on the back of his head. Several minutes passed before Adam resolved to shower but skip breakfast, if only to reach a compromise to move him forward. He did his best thinking in the shower and he needed to tame the twists and spikes that conspired to be his bed head.

Could a shower stall time? Reverse it? No, of course not—but his project could. It could do that and so much more: generate endless free power, check; recreate life, check. Adam's eyes widened … immortality, check. All he had to do was invent a revolutionary power source and use that energy to drive the next steps along the way to achieving time travel. Simple, right?

Adam didn't dare stick one toe out from under the covers. How did things get so out of control? How did one more day toward mid-life ruin everything?

Adam heard car doors open and close. He hurried outside to see what was going on.

"Wen?"

"Why are you out in your underwear?"

"Never mind me; where are you going?"

"To my parents'."

Adam sighed. He was afraid to ask why.

"What's that?"

"An updated will for the safety deposit box."

"Sorry, I can't. I'm running late." Wendy put the last bag into the trunk. She smiled. Everything fit.

She turned to hug him. Their embrace was shorter than either of them expected.

"Don't forget to take your blood pressure medicine."

She started the car and adjusted the mirrors.

"Wen—"

She was already out of sight. He lowered his head as he tried the front door. It was locked. Was it a good thing that his T-shirt and boxers matched? It would be a long walk to the office.

"Can't eat poetry," Adam chuckled as he approached a crossroad which reminded him of the path not taken. Sure, he would never write the next epic poem or the last chapter of a favorite character's life, but his family would never go to sleep hungry. His adolescent dream starved for the greater good.

Adam knitted his brow. He knew next to nothing about Mrs. Thomas beyond her obvious love for gardening. Her shrubbery alone would have won first prize, if there were such honors for suburban greenery.

Her husband? Adam once heard something very succinct about his career as a poet. Adam felt an uncontrollable urge to leave a bagged lunch at their doorstep.

Adam noticed a wayward bud on a nearby rose bush. Nature was reckless. Winter's knife would soon slice a killing cold upon this bed. Adam would renounce all science if that would grant this baby its blossom.

The sun peaked from behind a cloud. "It might be a warm day after all," he muttered as he walked on.

He stopped at the bank to put his will to rest. Adam received a strange look when he asked to access his safety deposit box. No, he didn't have his key, but they knew him. As he waited for approval, he scanned the list of bequeaths. He crossed out one name and wrote "Sam." He laughed. He always wanted to give Sam the bird.

Adam signed the log and placed the updated will in the box. As he turned to leave, the manager, the clerk, and all the tellers waved goodbye. They knew him well. He had no idea why the other customers were waving.

As Adam stepped out of the bank, he began to calculate the maximum sustainable temperature for the acquisition cycle. It would likely support another ten to fifteen degrees.

Adam smiled as he arrived, pleased to find Addy already working, well, eating in preparation for working.

"Good morning, Addy! How's my favorite time traveler?"

She watched him with an odd curiosity but said nothing.

"Good talking with you. Oh, Addy, can you adjust the shutoff for stage two? Move it up fifteen degrees."

"Fahrenheit?"

"Yes, Fahrenheit."

Adam disappeared into the small office on the left. The room, affectionally referred to as the closet, was full of trials and missteps. There was just enough room for a desk—

"Cold!" Yes, the chair was cold.

"Addy! Can you bring me the clothes from Table *A*?"

Addy reached for the key on top of the chassis to unlock the stage two door. The shutoff setting was just inside, on the left. Up fifteen. Done. There would now be a few more seconds before the acquisition cycle overheated and shut SAM down.

Addy avoided Adam for the rest of the day. He didn't trust her with any real work and she didn't need him anyway. He wasn't very helpful, didn't have any useful answers. Too many attempts to dig out necessary details ended in gawking silence … just like those college boys when she wore something tight.

She would work alone. With tons of information online, writing a phone app wasn't the issue. Interfacing with SAM's console would take some experimentation. She tapped her fingers on SAM's keyboard without actually depressing any keys. She needed to enter something if only to learn some nondeadly sequence. Maybe a transfer command with no options would fail safely. She typed 'transfer' and hit enter.

There wasn't an immediate response. Was SAM thinking?

"Error: 309: Stop wasting my time with incomplete information. Do you want to transfer a file? Maybe transfer whatever is on Table *A* to Table *B*?"

SAM had more personality than expected. She reentered the incomplete transfer command.

"Error: 309: Again. And deliberately this time. You're not Adam. Who are you and why are you messing about? Step away from the keyboard or I'll sound an alarm and they'll lock you away in a tower surrounded by a deep moat."

Addy laughed then grimaced, unsure of the appropriate response to a threat from something bolted to the floor. SAM's responses were canned, of course, but those references to a tower and moat….

She backed off. No need to go to war with a machine. She could use the incomplete command until she worked out the interface to the console. SAM would be the death of her unless she programmed a shutdown or kill command, something to put this monster down.

Addy tired of tinkering. She checked the clock. She could make better use of the next thirty minutes. Not here. Somewhere else, anywhere else. She mouthed goodnight as she tiptoed past Adam's door.

Adam pulled a bottle from his bottom right drawer. He had been saving this vodka for a special occasion. The oversized container seemed lighter than expected.

He frowned. He would need something really sharp to cut through this insidious web of considerations. After a drink or two, he found himself leafing through an ancient book. He stopped at a picture of a legendary sword known as *Raikiri*. The kanji characters beside the weapon seemed magical. As he traced the strokes with his finger, the mythical blade lifted off the page, swirling left and right, slicing through his bonds.

"Would Sam ever be a real man?"

His mind raced. How far would time bend? Would a second dimension be required? Would he modify matter or energy? He imagined performing surgery by deleting a tumor from the energy mix. Maladies out, enhancements in … middle age could be postponed by increasing height, reducing weight, adding a full head of hair.

Adam tapped the timeworn text. He knew what he had to do.

His eyes felt heavy. He turned his head to face east. This night, if only for an hour, he needed to dream facing the sea. Tomorrow he would set sail on a new and wonderful journey.

"Crap." He remembered locking himself out of the house. Tonight, he would dream facing the office door.

Clutch's Sweet Spot

ADAM hadn't exaggerated about the dire state of his life's work. The project was way over budget and he would need to share some significant success before he could hope for more funding. This would be his last chance. He had to find a way to tame the power curve. The problem was the energy ramp accelerated too quickly, outpacing the power consumption. The startup requirements were linear. However, once the beer began to spill, SAM's capacity went exponential before the conversion process could consume power at that rate. There was no where for that built-up energy to go.

"Besides boom?"

"Besides boom."

"Explain it to me."

"Sam, our energy equation is just old fashioned E equals mc squared. It's all about the mass. We can't drop a mountain from space, so we use math to simulate increasing mass. We divide a seed mass by increasingly smaller fractions. At startup, when we need linear energy to drive the initial dimension selections, we use everyday-sized fractions. But when we start the energy-to-matter-conversion process, our fractions are microscopic. We need the power of a singularity to consume any excess mass before it can accumulate and exceed the project's design dimensions."

"Before it explodes."

"Yes. And it's very, very hard to keep the energy creation in pace with the energy consumption. We need sufficient energy for our conversions but, if we don't redirect enough excess energy, we all die. Maybe not just those in the lab, maybe everyone in our dimension, maybe everyone in all dimensions."

"I'm beginning to see a slight problem here."

"So initially, when we are dividing by everyday fractions, we need only a small release valve for any overflow produced in our energy straw. However, when the fractions get itsy-bitsy, the small release valve won't cut it. We need a real heavy-duty overflow mechanism."

"Okay, so we need to convert the straw into a simple flute."

Ignoring Sam, Adam continued, "And finally, when we're consuming near infinite energy, we need to get Doctor Who serious with those fractions and have the appropriate singularity in place to consume any unused asteroid-sized chunks of matter before they can tear a hole in our otherwise inflexible straw."

"Plastic or metal?"

"It's a kind of metal, reinforced by a force field. We'll take the mass-exhaust and reroute it through a field generator to boost its strength."

"Okay, Adam, let me see if I have this right. We start with tiny pebbles which easily pass through. Then you hit the big red button?"

"Yes, we initiate the divide-by-zero technology."

"Then after you hit the big red button, those pebbles expand to the size of asteroids … which you have to suck through that straw—"

"Sam, I don't do the sucking."

Sam shook his head. He wanted to challenge Adam. Adam did do a lot of sucking. Maybe it was better not to derail this conversation. A key scientific contribution was on the tip of Sam's tongue. "Obviously, you don't do all the sucking. The … the—"

"The singularity does the sucking."

"Yes, Adam, you would have us believe the singularity does most if not all of the sucking—oh, and that the limitless energy is either consumed by the experimental energy-to-matter conversion, the untested turbo force field generator, or the so-called uncontrollable singularity itself."

"That's right, Sam … but the real issue is governing the fluxions."

Sam made a face.

Adam explained: "Having the proper mechanisms in place to control the rate and pace of the pebble-flow—"

"To the singularity."

Adam smiled. "To the singularity—so the rate can be properly regulated without starving the conversion process."

Sam tugged on his beard. "We need to find a way to release and tame the kraken."

Adam looked at his shoes. His socks didn't match. "We need a way to evacuate the excess energy flow while pinching the doughnut."

Sam rubbed his lower lip with his forefinger. "We have to pinch the doughnut?"

"At its core, at its exact core."

"But isn't the core a hole?"

Adam's face lit up. "Genius, Sam, pure genius."

"We have a solution? We don't have to let it rip and hope for the best?"

"Let it rip?"

"Adam, without my solution we'd be forced to hold our breath and hope for the best." Sam winked at Adam once, twice.

"I'm starting to feel a little claustrophobic in here."

"Take a deep breath. I could get you a paper bag—"

"No, I'm OK." Adam cocked his ear. "So…."

"So we divert the froth to the same whistle vent that the kill switch uses."

"We'd need a protective membrane to alter at exactly the right moment."

"Remove, not alter." Sam reached into his pocket. "When the matter flow changes from plenty of pebbles to way too many asteroids…."

Adam tapped his fingers. "Maybe a balloon would work."

"Try this."

"What's this?"

"You know what that is," Sam challenged with more winking, followed by an unfortunate series of hand gestures.

"A condom? Not a good idea."

"Adam, trust me. This baby is bullet-proof. It's better than ninety-nine of your *Luftballons*. It'll gather all the pebbles, bursting at the first sign of an asteroid." Adam wasn't convinced. Oh, it could work, it definitely could work, but it would be so hard to explain this usage to a scientific audience. "Adam, it's better than a balloon and it comes in many styles and colors."

Sam paused to seal the deal. "I've never had one fail on me."

"No asteroids?" Adam laughed. "Only pebbles?"

"Are you insinuating my froth isn't big enough?"

"Sam, you do realize we're using math, not beer. It was an analogy."

"Math? Not beer?"

Adam shook his head, up and down at first, then left and right. It was hard to say "not" while nodding in agreement.

Sam looked dejected. "Whoa, so you're telling me that doughnuts are like what? Like unwanted party guests? Like vegetables?"

"Of course not. I would never use those similes."

"No?"

"Doughnuts are nothing like Brussels sprouts." Sam made that face again. "Sam, I'm sorry, but we haven't used beer or doughnuts since the first prototype."

"Now you know why I never show up at work before breakfast."

Adam patted Sam on the shoulder. "I have something to confess."

"I think I'm gonna cry."

"RadioHut doesn't sell singularities. They used to … but not anymore."

"No singularities? No beer? No doughnuts? And you call me a bastard."

Uncertainty became fear as gray skies turned black. Must it be harmonic? Reverse the field? It could take a thousand trials to spark the glow of progress.

"Yes, but E has equaled mc squared since 1905."

Adam smiled as he recalled the conversation which inspired the near creation before him.

"Sam, come here. I need you."

"What's that? A boutique guitar pedal?"

"Settle down. I'll get you an Angry Sparrow for Christmas."

"Best guitar pedal ever. It's killer on bass too."

"Agreed, best pedal ever. Now can we talk about time travel?"

Sam nodded.

"Do you remember when I said we'd need to drop a mountain from space?"

"I think you said mountain range."

"The point was about having enormous mass."

"Life's always been all about the bass."

"Enough about the big *B*. I'm talking about the big *E*."

"And I raise you … the big *O*!"

"Sam, you're right!"

"First you need me, then I'm right! I've died and gone to heaven!"

"It's all about the big fat zero."

"Don't call her fat. She hates that. It reminds her of when she was little."

"We can't drop infinite mass from space, but we can divide by zero."

"What! I'm gonna pretend you never said that."

"We can divide a fixed mass by a very small fraction."

"I learned that in fourth grade: invert and multiply."

"We can incrementally create any mass by progressing through a series of shrinking fractions."

"Theoretically."

"We can approximate zero. I've done it in both my private and professional life."

"No, Adam, you can't."

"I can, too."

"You can't."

"Can."

"Can't."

"Can!"

"Can't! You realize I can out-can't you, like forever."

"Infinitely … infinite power."

"Infinite energy. You started this fight with the whole $E = mc^2$ thing. Don't start using power or will have to talk $P = F * v$."

"Get out of town!"

"Adam, please don't say that word. Your Pittsburgh accent sounds terrible when you say words like towel or town."

"Sam, you amaze me."

"Stop, I can't take any more praise. I'll burst."

"What are we going to call it? The big *E*?"

"No, let's call it the big red button."

"OK, Sam, you named it, so if anything goes wrong—"

"No, no, you can't blame this on me. Call it the little red button for all I care."

The return trip seemed a lifetime. She wasn't ready. She might never be ready.

"Where's Adam?"

"Hi, Wendy! How was your visit with—"

"Where is he?"

Addy pointed. "He's asleep."

"In the office?"

"He locked himself out."

"Ah, that's why he didn't answer my texts."

Addy followed Wendy. She didn't want to miss a thing.

Wendy whispered in Adam's ear.

"Sam?"

"Guess again."

"Oh, Wen, I had the strangest dream."

"About what?"

"Sam isn't dead."

"He isn't?" Addy's face lit up as she looked to Wendy for confirmation.

"They have a twin-like connection. Maybe he can—"

"No, I can't sense his presence."

Addy burst into tears.

"Adam, you're upsetting the poor girl."

Adam took Addy's hand. "I can't explain it, but I know he's alive."

Hope danced in her eyes. "You found a clue?"

"Not exactly, but give me a few minutes and I'll prove he's not a president, governor, or registered voter."

"What?"

"I think he jumped timelines. Maybe even into one that elected the same presidents."

"Is that likely?"

"More so than you might think. I call it the Star Wars effect."

"I'm going to regret this … what's the Star Wars effect?"

Adam smiled. He loved pretending to be the smartest person in the room. "When a society is young, it's obvious who is good and who is evil. The word 'empire' even sounds bad, right?"

"'Rebels' also sounds bad."

"That's why their full name is the Rebel Alliance. 'Alliance' is a politically correct term." Adam shook his head. His hair almost fell into place. "As time moves on, it's harder and harder to tell good from bad because power corrupts all republics."

"So everyone is evil?"

"From a certain point of view."

"And from another perspective, everyone is good?"

"No, human nature negates that possibility. We all see through our own eyes so someone, somewhere, is evil."

Wendy frowned. "What's your point? Evil's inevitable?"

"Of course not. You asked me about the Star Wars effect." Adam put his hand on his chin. "Why is it that the Jedi never perfected their selection process? So many Padwans turned to the dark side. They created their own worst enemies."

"So what does that have to do with Sam?"

"Only that our imperfect process may have landed Sam in the wrong timeline."

"Sam's in another dimension?" Addy's eyes shot fireworks.

"If I'm right, he's the first interdimensional traveler."

"Maybe the energy surge caused the transfer to skip to an adjacent timeline."

"Good point, Addy—like bumping the turntable."

"Like what?"

"Never mind. I'll search the adjacent timelines."

"Can we bring him back?"

"Yes."

"Yes?"

"Theoretically. Only two problems stand in our way: finding Sam's timeline and figuring out how to reflect a freak occurrence back on itself."

"We could modify the Select stage to use Sam's current location."

Wendy raised her hand to join in. "Rather than reflect a freak occurrence, could we reflect the existing window?"

"The current window projects light and sound; it doesn't transfer matter."

"What if we focused on receiving Sam's voice? Then we could tweak the parameters to get his image."

"Addy, I'm not sure that will help."

"Should we focus on adding matter transfer or creating a reflection?"

Adam thought for a minute. "Do we first create a one-way portal or a two-way video phone?"

"That's what I said."

"That's what she said."

"Yes, yes, that's what she said."

Addy labored for days without success. Wendy occasionally helped her with the math. Across the room, Adam worked alone.

"What's he doing?"

"It's best to let him be."

"Why isn't he helping us?"

"He likes to find his own path through a maze."

"I've seen him do that. He blows up walls."

Adam climbed high on a ladder, a true accomplishment in and of itself. He hoisted a reinforced external overflow mechanism and secured it in place.

"Adam?"

Adam turned white, nearly losing his balance. "Addy, you startled me!"

"What are you doing?"

"Fixing a key weakness."

"You're wasting time. Come help us validate our reflection parameters."

"I'm not much for mirrors. Reflections are better left to the young."

"Did you read that somewhere or do you make up that shit on the fly?"

"Language!" Wendy shouted from across the room.

"This new power flow control will find the sweet spot."

Addy's face went blank.

"The sweet spot, like on a clutch …when you aren't going forward or backward … and the car doesn't stall."

Addy's eyes growled at Adam. Why would he spew such nonsense?

Wendy nodded, confirming the existence of clutches and sweet spots.

"Addy, we need to control the energy to avoid skipping destinations. We don't want Sam to end up in the wrong place or with parts of him spread over multiple dimensions."

"Careful, Adam," Wendy intervened, "no need to speculate about unlikely outcomes."

"This power regulator mitigates those outcomes."

"So stop yapping and install it already."

Pinocchio's Island

SAM stretched his arms above his head and arched his back. His long dark hair rolled across his forehead, revealing steel blue eyes. He looked taller than his broad-shouldered five-ten frame, lighter than his actual 180 pounds. Such a shame that what was inside was still a child.

"Left sock first." Sam tried to ignore the controlling impulse. "No, not that sock, the one you touched first."

"This is why it takes us so long to get ready."

Sam checked his wallet for his room key. Nada. Not in his pockets. Not on the tables. Not on the floor. He looked for something to prop the door open.

A shoe?

He didn't have an extra shoe.

A pen?

The hotel pen was flimsy with a name on one side.

Sam looked at the blank wall above the desk. It seemed oddly familiar. He marked the wall with a single vertical stroke.

"Day one."

His stomach growled as he positioned the pen with his foot. Down the hallway he went, searching for food.

A ding. The far right elevator door was open. The car was empty. He pushed the lobby button, though one floor above or below might have been a better place to start. His hunger drove him along the sprawling lower floors, only to find all shops and restaurants barred.

He could ask for help at the front desk.

No, he wasn't going to ask for directions. He needed to get outdoors, break free from this eerie silence.

Finally, an exit sign. A shrill sound stopped him mid-stride. An emergency only exit? His hunger was an emergency.

He pushed through the doorway and froze. The trees were heavy with bats! Birds? He blinked twice before laughing uncontrollably: not bats or birds but thousands of bulbs perched on every limb. Sam marveled at the rows and rows of shimmering filaments spanning the grove from tree to tree, even connecting back to the hotel. One strand lit the narrow street ahead, revealing the path through the square.

Something big was about to happen here. But why was this prized loitering space empty? Was it the hour? When the clock struck five, would duty or desire drive thousands of workers down tight staircases and onto the street?

Sam approached the closest tree. He watched to see if the flock would take flight, pulling the bird-bulbs one by one off the limbs. He reached to touch—

"Hot! Hot!" Burned fingers were his penance for his "birdification" or whatever this was. Where was an English major when you needed one?

"Huh?" Sam grunted.

The young couple asked again. Sam couldn't make out all the words. Where was a Japanese major when you needed one? He was pretty sure they were asking him if he needed help, maybe if he needed directions.

"*Domo,*" Sam replied. It was enough. The well-intended natives moved on. They could not help a man unsure of what he hoped to find.

"Where did those two come from? Did they drop from the sky?" If not, he should have spotted them—walking along the well-lit path, stopping to park, emerging from the subway lair—long before they spoke to him.

"Food," his hunger interrupted, insisting he continue his search.

"The search for sustenance. Not a bad name for a quest." Sam laughed. Even he could see the absurdity of his situation. He was on a quest for food in Japan, as if no other country could serve raw fish, pickled ginger shrimp, and fried octopus in the same meal. Why not just go around the corner and eat at a deli like all the other middle-aged men? Or grab a soft pretzel and soda in the subway? A cheesesteak and beer?

It wasn't fair. He was missing all the important rites of passage.

Hold a second. How did he get here? Did he fly? How could anyone be on a plane for twelve hours and not remember it? Well, they do serve free beer on the upgraded ticket.

"Okay, stomach, quiet down."

Maybe this quest would go faster if he learned some Japanese.

"There!" Sam shook his head. "Why is the thing I'm hunting always in the last place I look?"

The single-story mall appeared as an endless winding string of interconnected specialty restaurants. Covered with a continuous roof, the black serpent wrapped around the block and into the next. Doorless entrances spotted its body. Smells of tempura and udon drowned in curry and cabbage.

Sam woke in the middle of the fourth floor hallway, lying next to an open door.

"Water, water."

The nearby room seemed empty. He stumbled in. The bathroom door was mostly closed. He pushed the door open. Also empty. His relief melted into melancholy. He felt so alone.

Did he want to find a stranger on the toilet?

He checked the sink and the tub. No running water. He returned to the hallway. The next room was locked. All the other doors were locked.

Down the steps he went. Third floor. Second floor. First. He found a maze of corridors and empty rooms. He searched the dining areas. The tables had place settings but no food or water. He staggered into the next corridor. The walls began to shrink as he took one step, then another. He was crawling before he reached the next hallway intersection.

"Left or right?" He dared not go forward.

"Right."

Right made sense. A maze could be escaped by always turning right.

He turned right and right and right again. He was crying by the time he saw the exit sign. He pulled himself upright and pushed hard.

The sun was warmer than expected. The trees seemed familiar, as did the streets. But these roads were empty.

He fell to his knees. He needed to sleep. He rubbed his cheek along the cool grass.

The sky turned bright yellow, then an odd blue, before fading to black.

Adam's hand hovered over the control panel. He slapped the big red button.

Shhhhikt!

A small ball of bluish white danced midair before settling on the wall behind SAM. The light grew larger and more brilliant, reaching the size of a tree-house door.

Dawn breached the wall of pale orange drapery.

"Don't move! Put your hands behind your back!"
The Nouveau Light Brigade surrounded his bed, poked him in the eyes.
"Tell us what we want to know."

Sam begged for ten minutes.
What had he done to deserve this?

"Were you the one who closed the curtains?"

"Yes, yes, just make it stop."

The lieutenant congratulated her team. Operation Daybreak infiltrated the only hole in the hotel's defenses.

Shhhhikt!

A loud garbled noise shook the room.

Sam hid under his pillow.

S sounds echoed off the walls.

"Is this a nightmare? Tell me you're not a snake."

"I am (static sound) ight."

"I wish I was alright. Did you rat me out?"

"I am the light."

"Jesus?"
"Sam! Guess again."
"Adam?"
"You need to find a way out."
"I tried that yesterday … what did I eat?"
Shhhhikt!
"Adam? Adam! Don't leave me with the snakes!"

Shhhhikt!
   "Sam, I'm back."
   "Good. Good. Though this time, I'm hoping for a little more than the ordinary haunt and run."
   "We need a plan."
   "Okay, plans are good, but here's a question before we get started."
   "Shoot."
   "Why are there so many cat videos?"
   "Sam, I'm here to—"

"Enough about you. All this me-me-me banter makes me forget what I'm trying to say."

Adam waited.

"Oh, right, I remember. I'm easily offended."

"Sam!"

"Don't look at me sideways."

"Have you been drinking?"

"Just water."

"What water? Show me."

"Maybe after my nap."

"Sam? Sam?"

A loud snore woke Sam. His fingers searched the night table, but he couldn't find his glasses. He pulled the clock closer to his face. 5:01.

A whisper of light peaked through a small gap in the curtains. He rose to his feet, stumbling. He steadied himself against the bed and again at the desk. His eyes grew big as he locked on a prize swaddled in bright orange mesh. He licked his lips, flashed tigerish teeth. How delicious its name must sound in Japanese. In seconds, one, two were gone. He toyed with the final morsel with dripping claws. He hesitated, becoming uncertain, remorseful as he swallowed the last bite.

"Were the drapes always that color?"

He struggled to say something funny as air carved from ice gnawed at his feet.

"Cold hands, warm … I can't even think of a good fart joke."

Maybe he would never be that funny kid from middle school. He looked like he had just peed himself.

"I probably don't even wear glasses."

He stretched before retreating under covers.

Fate soon released its sun-dogs. As their kisses thawed his muddled soul, he remembered the best fart jokes from a dozen books. His head was literally full of farts.

How could it be easier to project a lighter object? What does interdimensional projection even mean?

"Ready, Addison?"

"Tell me again why I'm the one?"

"I consulted the Oracle and I believe." Adam paused for effect. "You have the least mass."

Wendy frowned. She hated allusions to weight and sci-fi nearly equally.

"So what do I do when I get there?"

Wendy smiled. "Get his blood flowing."

Adam looked uncomfortable, trapped.

"Adam?"

"Let's keep things simple."

"I told you: KISS."

Addy blushed, then glared at Wendy. Yes, okay, she yearned to gnaw Sam's lips, but—

"What's going on with you two?" Adam shouted louder than intended. "Sam is in trouble."

Both women nodded sheepishly.

"There are unexpected side effects."

"Or he's been drinking."

Adam ignored his wife.

"Addy, whatever you do, don't touch him."

"So, you're telling me to KISS, but don't touch?"

Wendy burst out laughing. "Or don't tell."

Adam shook his head as he initiated the projection sequence.

Addy stood stiffly, biting her lower lip. She could hardly breathe.

Wisps of light wrestled free from overhead lamps, gathered midair. Faster and faster the ensemble twirled, round and round, pulsing brighter and louder.

Adam reached for Addy's hand. Her body glowed bluish white. She could feel the energy inside her, wrapping her molecules in light. Her heart raced in rhythm with the hypnotic vortex. Each second pulled her closer and closer, her body stretched as endless taffy sky.

Adam let go. The portal swallowed Addy, closing with an odd thud and zippering shout.

Shhhhikt!

Addy's hands flickered in and out. She hid them behind her back even though Sam laid glued to the bed, facing the wall.

"Sam?"

He didn't move.

"I can't stay. We're having a problem with the field."

"If you build it, they will come."

"Sam, we need to go."

"I'm a bit busy."

"You're busy?"

Sam smiled as he turned to prop up his head. "I have everything I need right here."

"Ass!"

"Well, now that you mention it."

"Sam, just tell me one thing."

"I'll tell you anything you want to hear."

"Does it come naturally or do you have to practice being the perfect ass?"

He laughed. She had him at ass. Maybe her initials were some combination of *P* and *A*. *P* for Perfect, or maybe Penny, Pamela? "*A* for…."

"Ass."

"Yes! This is a good dream, a damn good dream."

Addy raised her hand to slap him, but her body froze as she twisted her hips. Her projection jittered twice before cutting out completely.

A smile froze on Sam's lips.

Addy stomped back and forth, occasionally pausing to shout at the ceiling. It was a full two minutes before Adam dared speak.

"What's the matter?"

"He's such a jerk. He didn't even recognize me!"

"He's the two-year-old version."

"He acts like a two-year-old!"

Adam put his arms around her. "He doesn't know you yet."

"Of course he knows me."

"Not yet."

"Not yet?"

"Would you prefer karmic retribution over the Ouija board reading?"

Addy looked confused, then angry.

"Remember when you refused to push the big red button?"

Addy mumbled obscenities under her breath.

"That forced us to use the old data file."

"Old data file," Addy mocked.

"Don't worry. He'll love you more than life itself … once his beard grows in."

"A beard?"

"Take this." Adam handed her a tube of something.

"Why do I need—"

Adam smiled as he pressed the button.

Shhhhikt!

Sam's mouth was dry as he sat on the edge of the bed, watching his toes press heavily into carpet.

"Sam?"

He didn't look up but smiled, lifting his heels even higher. "I was dreaming about you."

Addy's eyes lit up, but she said nothing.

"I was looking deep into a well, wishing for you to be real."

"Sam, we need to go."

"I'm sorry I scared you off last time. I'm not used to having a tongue tied to my brain."

"You okay?"

"I'm fine, though a bit surprised. Turnaround time for wishes is incredibly unpredictable."

"Are you sure you're okay?"

"As good as anybody living the same day over and over again. At least it's my birthday."

"It's not."

"Look, I know when it's my birthday … though I can't find a piano anywhere."

"You don't play piano."

Sam frowned. "I've never tickled anything."

Addy hid her grin behind her left hand while twirling a ringlet with her right.

"Oh, dude," Sam thought out loud, "we could be stuck in that week between the holidays."

Addy removed a hair pin and tossed her head side to side. Glistening curls bounced against rosy cheeks.

"Oh, not a dude." Sam paused. "Your dream avatar seemed a little androgynous."

Addy arched her back. "Androgynous?"

"As I said, I was born earlier today."

"Maybe we are stuck in a loop."

Seconds passed. The silence begged Sam to speak.

"So, how's Adam coping without me?"

"He's okay, but we couldn't send someone with that much mass."

Sam laughed. "Did you just call Adam fat?"

"Stop, we have to find a way out." She smiled coyly. "He is a little chunky."

Addy reached for the door handle, but the door wouldn't open. "Any ideas how we get out?"

"Let me get my pants on!" Sam searched the bed covers for his jeans. "I need you to tell Adam something."

Shhhhikt!

"Tell him not to push the big red button."

Addy didn't respond. She had evaporated.

Sam sat at the small desk littered with crumbled notebook paper and closed his eyes.

Adam screamed as the vortex flashed open, yanking Addy's projection back into his dimension.

"Push the red button!" she shouted even before her feet touched the floor.

He slapped at the button without thinking.

The vortex roared and pulled her in. Her smile stretched between two worlds.

Shhhhikt!

Sam looked up from breakfast, but he wasn't the least bit startled. He had hoped for her return, this girl, this woman, this athletic red-head that no one would mistake for a dude—well, anyone who wasn't comatose. Though a bit too thin, it was nothing that a few chicken biscuits couldn't fix. Sam extended his hand.

"Call me Sam."

As Addy took his hand, her lips parted ever so slightly.

Sam traced the curves of her mouth with his finger. Or rather, he rambled on and on while wishing he had the courage to trace the curves of her mouth with his finger.

"So, while you were gone, I've been thinking." He looked deeply into her eyes. "You were wrong about me."

They lingered in the moment.

"Sam, we have to go." Addy squeezed the tube of sunscreen and rubbed two fingers across Sam's cheek.

"War paint?"

"You're sunburned."

"That's not the only place I'm…." Sam turned deadly serious. "I need to know something."

"What?"

"Where does all the lint go?"

"Huh?"

"All the severed buttons? The lost puppies? The fish when the water freezes?"

Addy couldn't answer. She wasn't prepared—

"Tell me, *PA*! Where do you go?"

"I don't like your calling me that."

"Did you just conjugate a possessive gerund?"

"I doubt it. I don't conjugate on the first date."

Sam smiled as he closed his eyes. He was sure she would conjugate on their first date.

"Sam?" If she tilted her head just so, he wasn't all that bad looking … but boy, did he smell. "Sam, wake up."

"Just five more minutes."

"You stink! You need a shower."

Sam opened one eye. "It's not me. It's my clothes."

"Then shower with your clothes on."

Her idea seemed so obvious. "You want to join me?"

Addy blushed. She hadn't meant to suggest such a thing, not on their first date, if this was a date. Or was he propositioning her? Say something, anything. "Soon, but without your clothes."

Sam grinned. "There's still one unanswered question."

"What question?" She absentmindedly put her hand on his shoulder.

He lost track of the … her touch was so arousing. "What question?"

"I asked you first."

"Oh, right … where do you go when you disintegrate?"

Addy wasn't sure how much to tell him. They'd already been here far too long. They needed to find a way out. "Nowhere. I just go poof."

His eyes were still locked on her.

"Grab your coat."

"On one condition."

"What?"

"Tell me your name."

"Addison, my friends call me Addy."

Addy pulled Sam along the hallway. He hardly noticed flight after flight as they hurried down thousands of steps. He was ecstatic to be holding her hand. An emergency bell cried out as she pushed hard against an exit door. The front of the hotel led directly onto an empty street. No honking horns, no jaywalkers, no roasting chestnuts up or down the block. A strange welcome for a city at dusk.

We crossed at the next block. Our pace was exceedingly brisk, perhaps motivated by some primal yearning for these unfamiliar paths to lead us to something real. I stopped for a second to acknowledge an inner voice urging me to look back before it was too late. A farewell glance revealed a fading bluish-white glow about the hotel door. A tug at my arm reminded me to keep up. My lungs wrestled humid air. I was unprepared, unfit for this adventure.

After two more blocks, the last warm light gave way to brooding night. A chill pushed its way into my coat. My fingers fumbled at a forgotten zipper. Had we ventured off the edge of the map? Maybe so, as all color seemed to fade from the cityscape, the sky now lined with worn wooden two-story buildings painted mostly black. Hazy panes revealed modest spaces. Here, vacant tables yearned to seat a dozen patrons. There, an empty bedroom waited for an unknown couple, an unnamed child. An entropic world with no hosts or patrons, no bustling chefs. Then it struck me. We were intruders, unwelcome at this in-between hour where no one sought work or food, where no life gathered. Block after block, only silence. A growing darkness pursued us, urging us to move more quickly.

We should return to the hotel. Look! At the next corner, a light. We hurried toward the welcoming glow. Mere moths, our eyes danced at discovering the door propped open. Be this bug zapper or corner grocery, we burst across the threshold, never fearing scorched flesh. Fate would be fate no matter what we might choose this day.

Heaven or hell? An impossible question as the myriad of aisles formed an untraversable maze. The displays of perfect nashi and ringo were well-orchestrated distractions ... till my nose caught the scent of mikan. I clawed my way deeper into the oasis, sinking my teeth into luscious flesh. My belly cried out as if finally free, finally whole. Many wide-eyed minutes slipped by with only a grunt or two.

I found myself waiting in a short line, arms wrapped round heavy glass, laden mesh bags. I put two thousand yen on the tray, returning a bow as I receive my change and receipt. I didn't speak. I know but a handful of Japanese words: good morning, good afternoon, good evening, please, thank you—and an odd phrase that warns against touching my mustache.

As I exited the store, I discovered my companion. I had forgotten I wasn't alone. After a few steps, a feeling overwhelmed me: I will never see this place again. We returned to the hotel by the most direct route, clutching our survival rations as the wind pushed from behind.

Sam woke to the sound of water. He smiled. He wasn't thirsty anymore.

"I've been here before."

"Yes, you have."

Her voice was familiar. Was this heaven?

"Osaka."

"What?"

"You're in Osaka."

"Right, Osaka. It was on the tip of my tongue."

"Dōtonbori, to be exact. Do you remember this bridge?"

Sam pushed himself to his feet.

"I do remember this bridge."

"Good."

"Where are the reflections?"

"What do you mean?"

"I see only light and dark."

"Sam, the lighter areas are the reflections."

"I mean there are no colors. No reds, no blues…."

"Many people are color-blind."

"No, Addy, you—"

"I'm not Addy."

Sam closed his eyes. He could trust nothing.

"Did you drink from the river or a nearby fountain?"

"I'm fine. Sorry to have bothered you."

"Maybe Dōtonbori doesn't agree with you."

Sam looked at the water falling from the fountains: white splashed on gray; gray enveloped gray.

"I don't remember you."

"I am no one, a voice inside your head."

"Why are you here?"

"You wished me here."

"Do you see colors in the water?"

"It's not time. They are not yet born."

"What are you saying? Color doesn't exist?"

"No, silly. Wait until it's a little darker."

"What? I haven't suffered enough?"

"See those buildings which line both sides of the river?"

"Of course."

"Which window glows red? Which sign casts blue light upon the water?"

"I don't understand."

"Then fly, fly away to another time. You are the one who spins this web."

Sam woke to the sound of tapping rain. He smiled. The clock read 5:01. He looked around to piece together a theory about the last eight to twenty hours.

Weird. The room seemed wrong. The curtains couldn't have always been that cruel shade of green. Sam took a deep breath to ready himself. What were the facts?

The other bed hadn't been slept in. He was alone.

The hair on the back of his neck stood on end, screaming an eerie warning. So not alone?

He sat at the desk, closed his eyes, counted to three. Reaching out with blind hands, his fingers brushed something, something soft, something round and cool to the touch.

"Breakfast!" His eyes flashed wide as he snatched up the prize. He pressed the mandarin to his lips. Oh, how he missed her!

Her? The orange was a she? No, but the person who made him whole was definitely a woman. His hands worked slowly. Bits of peel decorated the floor as if rose petals awaiting her feet.

"Slower."

He pealed more and more slowly as he slid lower and lower in his chair, until he landed on the floor.

"Meant to do that." He struggled to his feet.

He carved a vertical line on the wall above the desk with the hotel stick pen.

"Today is day one."

A Chicken or Egg Thingy

WENDY'S bed was full of peas. She was past thoughts of ever getting to sleep. Steam would soon burst from her ears.

"The diamond was never cleaned!"

Did she wake Adam? No, he would stay dead to the world till his own snoring roused him.

She dressed quickly. A loose edge of her misbuttoned top fluttered as she hurried downstairs.

The screeching radio startled her. She lowered the volume as she backed out of the driveway. The car was stuffy but she didn't open a window. The radio was still scanning through stations when she pulled into the parking lot.

Before the last fluorescent bulb reached full brightness, Wendy pulled a large stone from the soaking solution and patted it dry. Without the grime from stage two testing, the gem appeared flawless.

"Yesterday, here we come."

She smiled. Her mind was finally at peace. She would celebrate with a few hours sleep. She picked up her car keys, then set them down. A yellowed page beside the open log book caught her attention.

"Adam!" He was still obsessing over that design. She stuffed the sketch into his desk and scanned the log entries. The fourth one soured her stomach.

Death of original thought

The closer we get, the more uncertain I become. Will the outcome be worth all the sacrifice, all the past and future pain? Even when I

~~invent~~ we invent time travel, our success will only last a few seconds. Someone will travel back in time and rewrite history, force the world down an alternate path, creating a reality that doesn't depend on us, that didn't need me.

    Wendy picked up the diamond and put it in her coat pocket.
"No one will time travel today."

As she finished breakfast, Wendy noticed something odd about Adam besides his wearing only a T-shirt and boxers. "Adam, why do you have purple paint on your fingers? Wash your hands and get ready."

Adam abandoned his half-empty tea cup and hurried upstairs to dress. He grabbed a few loose notes and met Wendy at the car. Soon after arriving at work, Adam found the missing document in the bottom drawer of his desk.

"We're going to have to find a better place to hide you." He stared at the details of the drawing, then pulled back to see the big picture. "Immortality or immorality—is that even the question?"

Yes, Adam stored a digital copy of himself in SAM's memory during the preliminary human trial but only to validate that component. There could be no time travel if creating such a copy wasn't possible. As expected, it was feasible and mostly accomplished through brute force. If you can copy one molecule, you can copy them all. But in those early days of the project, Adam hadn't figured out how to reconstitute something as complex as a living being—or even an apple for that matter. He could verify the copy process by poring through the data, but he never generated enough power for successful energy to matter conversion. Months of testing yielded nearly two-thirds cup of applesauce but never a whole apple.

Adam wished he had accepted that failure faster. If he had, he would have focused on energy production as an independent component much sooner. Who knows, the next test might yield a steady energy stream—without demolishing the lab. Then he could not only teleport that Red Delicious apple, but he could clone himself whenever he wanted. Such a clone wouldn't remember anything that happened after the moment his essence was captured. He couldn't. He wasn't alive. He was a static image like a butterfly pressed into a keepsake album, except he wasn't sacrificed. He was photographed, so to speak, and a copy of that very detailed image was stored in a massive array of next generation NAND nonvolatile flash.

Adam's clone remained untouched for almost two years. Even after another decade, the clone's image would remain ageless and ready to take flight. So this could have been about immortality, but it wasn't. It wasn't even about time travel anymore. Adam had a new goal. His true objective had always been about Sam. Whimsy and glory got in the way just as unnecessary complexity could have added several lifetimes to the project.

Sam needed to be his own person. After the impossible power requirements were satisfied, a few highly intelligent subroutines would sort out the Sam bits from all the other zillions of bits. Adam cringed at the thought of the trials necessary to find every needle in every haystack. He envisioned piles of mutilated bodies.

Adam ran for the bathroom but didn't make it. He could never stomach the brutality of creating such a monster. He survived by immersing himself in the myriad of biological and psychological riddles that plagued the project's progress.

After adding the Sam-specific psychosocial attributes into a relational database, Adam realized physical characteristics were arbitrary. Sam didn't need to have any of Adam's limitations. Of course he had to be human—and Adam didn't want to add risk by trying to integrate two clones—but the actual body could be tuned. Something as simple as reducing the percentage of fat cells would be a straight-forward tweak.

Writing a routine to map those attributes to the cloned datafile would be tedious, but a conservative rule of thumb would be to include any parts that can't be ruled out. It would be far easier to hold back the obvious Adam-only bits than to extract an exact model of Sam.

Adam picked up the log book and wrote:

transfer -file Adam.app -to TableB -mod !Adam.specific -mod minus.10

The "!Adam.specific" modification is key as it will screen out those characteristics unique to Adam.
The "minus.10" modification will trim 10 pounds of middle-aged fat—or should weight be described in kilograms? Ten kilograms.
Can we make it fifteen? Fifteen, do I hear twenty?

Adam spread a dozen pages across his desk. He wanted to see everything at once as a way of coalescing the fragments into a cohesive design. When he stood up to get a better look, he spotted a small silver-colored beveled ring.

"What's that?"

"I don't know."

"Then throw it out."

"I might need it."

"Then put it somewhere safe."

Adam sighed. "By the time I know why that ring came into my world, my odds and ends container will be overflowing."

"So get a new bin."

"How would I know which special place holds a particular thing?"

"Get a bigger container."

"Really, Sam? Put all my things in one gigantic container?"

"Oh, right, you'd search and search but never find what's really important."

Adam's face turned troubled. "Sam, do you have a bucket list?"

Sam flashed his not-sharing-something-so-personal face. He was tired of being alone.

Adam placed the ring on an open spot on his desk and reached for a pencil. He quickly sketched a composite design and labeled it "Immortality 2.0." Adam heard Sam but couldn't focus on his words as he was busy wondering if off-the-shelf memory could contain all the necessary data.

"Adam, are you listening to me?"

"You were going on about broadening something."

"I need to experience something truly novel."

"Let me get my Sam decoder ring."

"I'd like to travel and write a book."

Adam laughed. "I was sure you were going to say something about falling in love."

"Oh, okay. I guess I can do that too." Sam's eyes softened. "Do you think anyone could ever love this mug?"

"People say we look like brothers."

"Whoa, Adam, no need to hit me with both barrels. Just say no when you mean no."

"Where do you want to visit?"

"I have some unfinished business in Japan."

"Now we're getting somewhere. What will you write about?"

"Something that will make people change before it's too late."

"A bucket-list novel."

"A novel to end all bucket lists."

"Right. Do you mean your novel would be the last item on bucket lists … or that, after reading your novel, there'd be no need for bucket lists?"

"There you go, Adam, overthinking everything."

"It's just that you've never been this serious about anything. Year after year, you've been a lump of clay. And now you're a shiny terra-cotta vase."

"You say vase; I say vase."

"Sam, you always were a little on the snooty side."

"What's it called when something's not quite as bright and shiny as it thinks it is?"

"A reproduction. Know anyone who's a copy?"

"Now who's the funny one."

"Will the real comedian please stand up?"

"I win. I'm already standing."

"Oh, I thought you were sitting."

Sam huffed and puffed. "I'll get you back, Piggy … when you least expect it."

"Now that everything's back to normal, what were you saying?"

"A novel to end all bucket lists."

"Yes, wonderful, a novel. About your travels in Japan?"

"With a twist or two. I like surprises."

"You like to gamble."

"I'd like to take my chances on something really big, like a trilogy, like *Gone with the Wind*."

"*Gone with the Wind* isn't a trilogy."

"It felt like one."

"It does have an intermission."

"With just enough time to hit the snack bar."

"Oh, Sam, I love halftime."

"Remember … empty before fill."

"I learned that at a doubleheader in Three Rivers Stadium."

"Did Pittsburgh win?"

"I don't know. I got stuck in the line for the men's room."

Sam shook his head. He never expected to live his life as a straight man.

"So, Sam, why a trilogy?"

"Well, for one thing, a trilogy has two halftimes."

Adam made an alteration on his diagram, changing the angle of some very long tube. He wanted more for Sam … if only his resumé didn't read TBD, page 1 of 1.

Adam tapped to get Sam's attention. "Wendy wants to go to the zoo."

"I don't do zoos."

"Come on, think of it as visiting family."

"I can't. It's not fair." The grief in Sam's eyes was real.

"What's not fair, captivity?"

"It's not fair to the giraffe."

"The giraffe?"

"To be so close to the hyena."

"Maybe that hyena's an up-and-coming comedian."

"Maybe he's an ass."

"Maybe they're friends."

"Would you be friends with an ass?"

"Well—"

Sam looked away. He had heard enough.

"We can take our grandchild."

"Grandchild? Isn't your daughter fifteen?"

"So?" Adam checked his watch. It told the year as well as the time.

"So isn't your one and only job to prevent her from having your grandchild?"

Adam panicked. "It was Wendy's therapist who suggested the zoo."

Sam's eyes got big. He knew Adam was hiding something. "Therapy?"

"Yeah, she just started. Some of her friends were going."

"It's a social event? Let's all get in a car and visit a therapist?"

"Pretty much. She got a great group rate."

Why was Adam pushing this lie so hard? Was he dropping a pin to help us navigate this timeline?

"Adam, I figured it out."

"You did?"

"Was it the therapist in the group session with the candlestick?"

"Good guess. Check this to see if you're right." Adam passed him a slip of paper.

The note sent chills up and down Sam's spine. "We should hurry. The zoo closes at dusk."

Sam unfolded Adam's note. It made no sense.

"Hospital, tomorrow, 9:00 a.m. Bring a spoon."

Maybe the note was intentionally vague.

"Maybe I shouldn't have read that note out loud."

Why would the hospital be safe? Were they only watching the lab? Did "spoon" mean "weapon"? He had twelve hours to figure this out. Sam searched one pocket, then another, but found nothing … not that bringing a penknife to a space-time-continuum fight would be of much use.

Sam picked up a pen. It would have to do.

He would reconstruct the current timeline with a series of sticky notes: green to chronicle timeline anchor points, yellow to highlight black cats or other out-of-context clues, and red to flag unresolved time bombs.

Sam yawned as he positioned the last note. He had been fighting sleep for the last nine hours. He took another bite of candy before tapping his fingers near a cluster of red notes. If he were looking at a map, he would avoid this neighborhood at all costs. What green or yellow events led to those streets? Was that a loop? He was about to pull the thread that would unravel this mystery. He smiled at the thought of never waking up beside a fountain again.

Sam woke shortly after nine. Something was stuck between his teeth. He pulled out a bit of orange flesh. Couldn't be. Something was wrong. He hadn't eaten a real dinner. He hadn't eaten fruit … only chocolate.

"Shit!" He was late. He reached for his keys but found only a penknife. He rushed to his desk. The crime-scene-reenactment notes, all his insights—were gone.

He left without locking his door, without pulling it shut. It didn't matter. Nothing mattered in a world that stole from you as you slept.

Wendy had about fifteen minutes before the first bell. She went over her notes as Addy watched dozens of tired faces dribble into homeroom. Addy understood. Anything that started before 8:00 a.m. deserved resentment.

Why did everyone look so young?

The bell.

Wendy welcomed the students. Some seemed preoccupied, scouring desks for that first period book, lost assignment, or hair brush. Most were facing front, watching Addy's every move. Very few would learn anything about applying everyday math.

"All our temperatures use the Celsius scale. So when we need to adjust one of the temperature sensitive systems, like the laser strength or the emergency shutdown trigger, we convert our target Fahrenheit temperature to the appropriate Celsius value. Addy can you give an example?"

Addy was afraid to speak. Some of the older boys looked like they were about to explode.

"Addy?"

"Sure, Ms. Driver." Addy swayed as she moved forward. Her hair, her hips, her—

A wave of moans stopped her advance. Maybe it was better if she stayed put.

"Say we want to make a fifteen degree Fahrenheit change to a regulator."

The whole front row was mouthing the word regulator.

Addy looked away. "To convert a Fahrenheit temperature to degrees Celsius, we take the current temperature setting minus fifteen. Wait. Ms. Wendy, what did you say?"

"Right, Addy. All SAM's temperature readings are in Celsius, so we calculate the desired change and convert to Celsius."

Addy's face lost all color. "I killed Sam."

A horde of happy hands caught Addy before she hit the floor.

Adam opened a window into an alternate dimension with the push of a button.

"Places, everyone."

"Adam, we're the only ones here."

"And action!"

"So I was presorting laundry when—"

"You were what?"

"Presorting laundry, when she—"

"She?"

"My wife."

"Sam, you're not married."

"Addy and I eloped last Friday at 3:45. I was going to tell you after the show. Anyway, I was presorting laundry when my wife called to me."

"3:45?"

"We made it to the justice of the peace at 3:30, were married at 3:45, and finished our honeymoon just before 4:00."

"Where was your honeymoon, a taxi?"

"No, of course not." Sam looked down at his shoes. "A roadster."

"My roadster?"

"Unfortunately, we got stopped for indecent exposure—"

"You were driving?"

"No…."

"Addy was driving?"

"No one was driving. We were in the back seat."

"Liar! A roadster has no back seat!"

"Okay, so we took her convertible, not the roadster, big deal." Sam took a deep breath. "I had just started presorting laundry when Addy called to me. She wondered why my bath water was still in the tub."

"Bath water?"

"I had forgotten to drain the tub, but she accused me of doing it on purpose."

"Like in case you needed to presoak something?"

"That's what she said!"

"Sam, does she trust you?"

"Well, I did beep the horn during the honeymoon."

"You honked for fifteen straight minutes?"

"No, only when something important happened."

"You're not really married, are you?"

"No, but I did disconnect the car horn just in case this weekend looks promising."

A cold breeze swirled as the women returned. The men froze, caught in the act, knees awkwardly bent, elbows pointing in inconceivable directions as if dropped from a height.

"Sam, you should have said 'alien' abduction."

"What are you two up to?"

"Spitballing comedy sketches."

Wendy rolled her eyes. The positions of their knees and elbows still made no sense whatsoever.

"Physical comedy?" Addy offered.

Sam nodded. "At least we don't have paper wads stuck to the backs of our necks."

Adam shrugged his shoulders. "Sam, I wish you had said 'stuck to our foreheads.'"

"But when the delinquent shoots the kids in front, the spitballs stick to the backs of their necks."

"And in hair. That's the worst."

"So, I was right?"

"No, remember you're on the Big City Stage with thirty-seven spotlights shining on every dimple of your face. So, Sam, if we go with forehead, you can use the reveal of the spitball as a send-off."

"Big City Stage, where's that?"

"Downtown. I guess it's called Big City Music Hall now."

"But Adam, I don't want to learn to play an instrument."

"Not even guitar?"

"Well, maybe jazz guitar."

"Cool. What color?"

"Big City Music Hall is a serious place with serious people, right?" A smile curled from the corner of Sam's mouth. "So, I'd go with Daphne Blue or Red Paisley Flames, and end the first set with a blues tune."

"Good. Smile as you roll into the next joke."

"I'm approaching a large oblong table in the center of a bright room."

"Yes, yes, love the suspense."

"Everyone keeps looking at me."

"At you?"

Sam narrowed his eyes. "Yes, me."

"Come on. The setup has to be believable."

Sam tapped his fingers against his fierce red flame. "A person … a person walks up to a craps table and puts all their money on white."

"Nope, can't bet white."

"Roulette?"

"Red or black. Think poker."

"I've seen green cards, though I'm not a fan."

"You're right. Decks can have blue and green suits."

"I was once surprised by a large print deck in a tournament. Somebody said it was probably left over from a dealer's game."

"Was that a joke?"

Sam looked off into space, biting his lower lip.

With her hands in her back pockets, Addy shuffled over to Sam. Her jeans fit very tightly.

"Hello in there."

Sam could read her body language—one of the skills gleaned from countless hours at the poker table. "Hello out there."

"You guys get any big ideas while Wendy and I were out?"

"Of course."

Addy smiled coyly. "Like what?"

"Show her, Adam."

Adam raised the infinite energy pedal. "Our big red button."

Sam looked away, feigning humility. "We solved the variance issue."

Addy looked to Adam for confirmation. The comedy director slash wingman nodded, though unsure where Sam was heading.

"You see, Addy, advancing through scientific trials requires the introduction of a single change."

"So that you know the true impact."

"Right, but it's hard to keep all the other stuff from changing. Unexpected permutations cloud the outcome. A trial might succeed due to the intended variation or because the environment had a lower concentration of dust particles. It's easy to misinterpret false positives and chase down a blind alley. Sum variance is a killer."

Addy's lips parted in awe.

"Since we can push around infinite energy, we don't need no stinking variants."

"Sam, can I clarify?"

"Well, Adam—" Sam looked dejected as Addy turned to face Adam.

"When you have a big enough E, you don't need to predict the energy required for time travel—and you don't have to correct for any variances. To hell with gravity, vacuums, and subject mass. Hell, to hell with dust."

"Big E's lead to big O's." Addy shook her head at Sam's childishness.

Adam continued without breathing. He was on a roll. "How long would it take to properly estimate E? And during that time, what variables have changed? Do we start over and try again?"

"Hell no!"

"Right! Why waste power testing all the variations?"

Addy smiled.

"All we have to do is watch Table B. No apple yet? Add more E. Not yet? More E."

"Not O?" Addy teased.

"And how do we get infinite energy?"

"The big red button!"

"Look at the time. Which should we tackle first? Adjusting the stage two targeting laser or adding a redundant circuit to the acquisition equation?"

Adam's face turned deadly serious. "Which is the chicken and which is the egg?"

Wendy averted her eyes. "Why do you ask?"

"Simple deduction. To know which comes first, you need to identify the chicken."

The team drifted in confusion as if gravity had been turned off. Wendy tried not to throw up by staring at the floor. Addy leaned her head back to stop a nosebleed. Sam was Sam, spinning in circles.

"OK, let's use a poverty example instead."

Addy protested. "What does poverty have to do with evolution?"

Wendy stomped her foot. "What does evolution have to do with anything?"

The women eyed each other. Wendy had several inches on her, but Addy's martial arts training made her a two-to-one favorite.

"As I was saying, a mother has two children, both are born poor but one gains great wealth. Is it child A or child B who breaks the cycle of poverty?"

Wendy called out A as Sam shouted B.

Addy shuddered. "Why can't the siblings share the money?"

"Semantics," Sam asserted.

"Semantics?"

"I thought you were the English major."

Addy's eyes narrowed. Sam kept his distance. Adam looked astonished.

"I hired an English major?"

Addy cowered behind SAM's chassis.

"Chickens never go first." Adam opened the stage two door and reached for the laser adjustment knob.

"No!" Wendy screamed as the undirected laser arced across Adam's chest, slicing bone and searing flesh.

Addy hit the kill switch.

Sam fell to his knees. Why hadn't he warned Adam the diamond was missing?

Addy dialed 911 as Wendy reached into her pocket.

Dig Deeper

SHE shuttered as she watched death circle Adam's bed. Hopelessness drove its fingers deeper and deeper into her head. She too would be lost if she stayed another minute.

"Addy, since you're up, can you get me a drink?"

"What? You want a drink?"

"I need something to keep me awake." Wendy pulled a partially crocheted hat from her bag. Her hands moved so quickly.

Addy lowered her head as she walked out.

The ride home never registered in Addy's consciousness. She found herself outside her apartment door, searching her pockets. She seemed disappointed when she discovered her key.

The door stopped halfway; she stepped back and kicked the obstacle against the entry wall. She raced room to room, turning on every light. She mumbled as she paced in front of the couch. Was it her fault? Four steps, turn. She reached for the TV controller, flipping through channels while pounding her feet; the rhythm soothed her, until it didn't.

She searched the refrigerator before settling for warm milk. She tapped her fingers as she looked through the glass, waiting for something to happen. She went to bed without taking a sip.

She sighed as she turned and turned again. Just as she filled her lungs to scream, she heard something.

"Couldn't be."

She listened carefully. Which of the two books on her nightstand would be the first to speak? A minute passed. Two. Still nothing.

She opened the larger book to the bookmarked page: 482. She smiled. She was nearly halfway through the quantum physics tome. She read each page as if her life depended on it.

"Another reference to that damned cat!" She put the book down. "Even Adam knows Schrodinger wasn't serious about that paradox." She turned off the light and closed her eyes.

An image started to form in her mind.

"Adam?"

She couldn't tell if he was breathing.

"Adam?" She moaned as she tugged at her hair.

She retraced the events leading up to Adam's injury.

"Was it my fault?"

"You weren't even in the car."

"Mom?"

"Sleep, honey; you've had a rough day."

"Maybe I did something wrong. Maybe I—"

"You didn't force the bourbon down his throat."

Tears formed in Addy's eyes as her mother knelt at her bed.

"Baby, I'm worried about you."

"I'm okay, Mom. I still have my work."

"Yes, it will be even more important after he's gone."

Everything went dark. She could hear the sound of rain.

Lights were approaching.

The vehicle swerved as it passed her.

"Slow down, you fool!"

She recognized the sedan as it approached a sharp turn.

"Hit the brakes!"

The car didn't slow.

"Dad! Hit the brakes!"

The car flipped before disappearing over the cliff.

Addison woke when she heard the explosion. She turned on the bedroom light.

"It was just a dream," she assured herself, pressing her hand to her racing heart.

After many deep breaths, she reached for the smaller, more colorful book on her nightstand.

Addison peered into the cave. She could see nothing, but the smell was undeniable. She lit her torch. This was the way to the dragon's lair.

She walked on till she came upon a large empty chamber. Dusty brown walls curved as far as the eye could see. A house could fit—

"Ah-ha!" She discovered an exit angling off to the left and a second one nearby. Cobwebs draped the smaller opening whereas the right path seemed clear ... though the ground leading that way was rough, carved by a century of pain.

"Something dragged a thousand bodies down that hole."

The voice inside her head begged her to turn back. She did not, even when she heard bones crunching underfoot.

That was her first mistake.

She pressed on, but the path had no end. She stopped to rest. That was her second mistake. The dragon slept a stone's throw from where she placed her sword and shield.

Addison yawned. She looked so tired.

She barely reached her shield before the dragon's breath lit the cave. Flames burst round the edges of her buckler.

"Should have brought a bigger shield!"

That wasn't her third mistake. Leaving her sword behind as she stopped to brace against flame after flame ... that was her third mistake.

Addison heard someone sobbing. She tried to console her, but Addison's hand passed through her mother's shoulder.

"Mom?"

"He misses you."

"Who?"

Her mother laughed. "But maybe you don't miss him."

"Please don't laugh. I feel terrible."

"Poor child, death does not stop destiny."

"Mom, what are you saying?"

"Take this."

"I don't need a shovel."

"Dig!"

"I don't want to d—"

"Dig!"

Addison was knee deep before she looked up.

"Deeper!" her mother shouted as a patch of skin fell from her face.

We All Hate Hospitals

ADAM took a deep breath, in through his nose, out through his mouth. He could tell by the position of the sun and the smell of scrambled eggs that it was nearly time for breakfast.

"I'd thought you'd never wake."

"How'd you get here?"

"Bus, train, usual stuff."

"Unlikely." Adam's eyes looked so glassy.

"Truth is overrated."

"Sam, how did you open an interdimensional window without the lab equipment?"

"Don't sweat the details. Maybe I traveled four hundred years into the future and borrowed the wrist watch version of your invention."

"Sam, I'm worried about you. Do you have any hobbies?"

"Like what?"

"Painting, playing a musical instrument, something you'll be able to do your whole life."

"I'm not into loud or messy things."

"I started painting after Granny passed."

"I remember." Sam sat on the bed. "When did you last play your trumpet?"

Adam started to smile, then flinched. "At my brother's wedding—"

"Which one?"

"The younger one. I was so nervous."

"You did fine … and the videographer did a really great job of editing out—"

Adam sighed. "My brothers always had my back."

"Adam, are you okay?"

"I used to hit high *D* without thinking."

"Maybe we should check what drugs they're giving you. Let me see your chart."

"Seriously, Sam, you need a hobby."

"Wow! You're on a ton of antibiotics!"

"Typical protocol for a lightsaber injury."

"Look, Adam, I have to go."

"As Dad used to say, thanks for leaving."

Adam's stomach rumbled. His apple juice sat untouched.

Adam raised his bed to a more comfortable seating position and swallowed dutifully. The nurse left in a blur of white. He meant to ask something, but the only words he could parse belonged to someone else.

A stray spring stabbed his back. As he rubbed away the pain, he wondered if furniture designers were required to add extra bits of metal to minimize hospital stays.

How long had he been in recovery? The accident happened on a Monday. It was Tuesday. A week Tuesday, his eighth morning on a please-discharge-me mattress.

Maybe it wasn't Tuesday. Adam had trouble keeping track of time. The evenings lingered; the mornings jumped ahead. He suspected a strong correlation between the passage of time and the frequency of his pain medication. Maybe he would decline his next pill. He didn't need to suppress the pain as much as he needed to get back to work.

"What's that?" A pad of drawing paper with a purple ribbon and a bow of nearly the same hue. Adam wondered if certain blues were destined to steal the snap from companion reds, making the joining a bit dull, a bit....

Was the gift from Wendy? She once brought ice cream to the computer lab. The mint chocolate chip wasn't the only thing melting that night. Had it been twenty years since that kindness? He searched his memory: the bookmark, the hug at the top of the stairs before break....

There must have been hundreds if not thousands of other examples; yet, he could not recall her last tenderness. Adam pulled the violet ribbon and removed the first sheet of paper. He would write their next chapter.

After a few attempts to write a reasonable opening, Adam crossed out every word. Then, as he wrote SAM 2.0, something miraculous happened. The color in his face returned; a series of swift lines converged effortlessly as if guided by another's hand. The pencil swirled and tapped, marking the intent of each design element and noting actual working parts. He finished just as the medication took hold. His eyelids grew heavy. A familiar warmth wrapped his shoulders. He smiled and closed his eyes. He could hear a beating heart. He could feel its slow and steady rhythm.

"I told you. It's rock steady."

"Another child? Without a learner's permit?"

"A slow heartbeat is a boy. The doctor said he'd bet on it."

"One boy, right? Not twins?"

Months passed with lots of belly flaunting. Then one day, off to the hospital they went for a long and difficult delivery. Honestly, Wendy did most of the really hard parts. For Adam, the only truly excruciating moments were when Wendy shared the strongest contractions. Who would have thought a 120-pound person, clothed in nothing but an untied hospital gown, could squeeze with such force? Still it wasn't easy to repeat "breathe" for like nineteen hours straight. And all those how-could-you glares, especially in the last hour or two, can leave scars for life.

They named their son James after Adam's childhood spy persona. There was something really special about naming your boy after a secret agent. Some dared say the boy's name was a tribute to Adam's boss, but that was nonsense. Who would name their child after an authority figure, someone who could influence future income?

Can you love a child too much? Adam once filmed a forty-minute nap and sent a personalized copy to every family member. At minute twenty-six, Jim yawned. Should such a parent be institutionalized or at least blacklisted against future purchases of blank video media?

Before long, Jim was walking and talking, running and writing. He found his voice in a short story about string. Adam hadn't foreseen how wonderful that memory would now feel. He longed for a copy of "Ode to String" for his office wall.

Childhood escapes us all, our stories get lost, our songs are no longer sung.

Summers once meandered from sunup to sundown, from backyard to ball field—but now time refused to kick back, to simply be with us. There aren't enough hours for all the work meetings and all the family sporting events. Our towns have become home bases, places to rest before running out again.

We used to play in our neighborhoods. We didn't commute to playtime. We didn't have uniforms or referees or hundreds of spectators. And why doesn't that coach teach those children how to play their positions? They're like a pack of wolves chasing a wounded ball. Should such a game even be called soccer?

Somehow only Adam's son knew how to play his assigned role. When an opposing player dared to enter his left-back zone, Jim nailed the ball with a booming kick! Were the other children just not listening? Is there some innate flaw which makes humans ignore rules and structure, even laws? Let he who has not exceeded the posted speed limit cast the first stone.

Still it's sad to think our children might make our mistakes. We should warn them somehow—right, like a teenager would ever accept advice from a well-meaning guardian. It might be easier to invent time travel than persuade a young adult to follow the prescribed yellow brick road. We don't write their screen plays or choose their friends. We don't live in their time or think with their words. We don't own their souls. We stumbled, sure, so maybe we have to let our children stumble along their own paths.

Adam closed his eyes and it was spring. The late morning sun scoured the pavement, spreading warm fingers up and down the building's facade. Light poured through windows in search of young faces. The gusting wind turned pages as students crammed for exams.

Adam remembered the stiffness of the desk chair and straightened his back. He felt trapped between the exterior wall on his left and the built-in armoire on his right. He couldn't catch his breath. He was sweating.

He stood and pressed his palms against the thick center pane. He pushed harder and harder. Everything went blank.

"Addy?"

"Not cool, dude."

"Sam?"

"Open your eyes and you'll be back in the land of the living."

Adam peeked out one eye. The room was too bright. "Sam, where are you?"

"I'm where I always am."

Adam opened both eyes and he was back in his office. He frowned. Not much had changed in twenty years. "I need a vacation, maybe a drink. What time is it?"

"Half past a freckle."

"Wow, Sam, that comment dates you."

"Dates us … but who would date us, right?"

"Have you seen Addy?"

"Never you mind Addy. How 'bout a game of chess?"

"No."

"A road trip? AC?"

"It might be fun to get away for a couple of days."

"If only I had the money…." Sam looked around the room.

"You can buy in for as little as forty dollars."

"If I wanted to be short-handed. Even if I go all-in, I won't scare anyone."

"I'm not sure about that—"

"Look Adam, I'd come in on the big blind, so two hands later I'm down to thirty-seven bucks."

"I too won't defend my blinds until I get a feel for the table."

"By the time I get a decent hand, my bet won't mean anything. Someone's gonna call my lousy all-in bet."

"You can't always wait for a good hand." Adam smiled. "I once won with 7-2."

"You were the big blind and got lucky."

"If you're not going to get lucky, why even play? You'd be better off investing in the market."

"You got me, Adam. I thought you were going to say I'd be better off playing slots." Sam laughed. "I can do some real damage when I have a big stack in front of me."

"You certainly don't want the guy with rags to catch two pair on the flop."

"Poker might be the perfect game."

"So true, Sam. The world could be spinning out of control, but Hold'em will always deal you another hand."

"Till the blinds bleed you dry."

"That's the funny thing about life. Your intuition tells you to wait for a good hand … but, if you muck too much, you'll run out of time."

"Poker is like life. They're the same really."

"Give me Hold'em or give me death."

"Adam, have you been drinking?"

"Me? No. Just a little." Adam refilled his glass, refusing eye contact.

When Wendy returned to the hospital, she found Adam snoring. A pencil graced his right hand. She smiled, pleased to have remembered his B pencils from home. Something about the softer feel gave Adam great pleasure.

Then she saw it, a sheet of drawing paper hidden in the food tray debris. As she studied the boxes and revealing comments, her face beamed. She grabbed for her phone and keys. Once at the bank, she retrieved the initial version of the SAM design from the safety deposit box. She overlaid the two drawings and couldn't contain her joy. She laughed and cried. She was so relieved and so proud. Adam was still the man she married. Why had he hidden his true intent from her? How did she not guess his secret?

She rushed to the lab and pressed the big red button. Sam was in bed. He looked oddly elated, then extremely guilty.

"Sam, you won't believe this!"

"Trust me. I'm more gullible than you think."

"This is an early version of Adam's design."

Sam studied the drawing for a few seconds. "Seriously, immortality?"

"That's what I thought."

"He must have passed out before he finished it."

"He told me he stopped drinking."

"From exhaustion. He passed out from exhaustion."

"And this one—"

"What's this?"

"A revised version."

"I recognize this! We discussed this design at the bar." Wendy glared. "At the lab, late one night at the lab."

"I found it at the hospital earlier today."

"Adam has a good memory. That's definitely our invention."

"All this time, it was never about prolonging his life."

"He just wanted me out of his head."

"Sam, isn't he something?"

"I've been saying that for years. How's he doing? How's his vertigo?"

Wendy's face went blank. "What vertigo? Why are you holding a spoon?"

"Um?" Sam hid the spoon behind his back. "It's Adam's?" Sam cleared his throat and lowered his voice. "It's Adam's."

Sam remembered how Adam couldn't recline below forty-five degrees without his eyes darting back and forth, without nausea overwhelming him.

"No vertigo? How was the aneurysm discovered?"

Wendy's eyes widened. "Aneurysm?"

Sam stared crosseyed at the tip of his nose. The world went blurry. He could barely hear the buzz of Wendy's voice. Did he jump the gun? Did events pan out differently in this dimension?

"Sam, tell me the truth."

"Who's to say what's real in any given minute?" How was he aware of events from multiple dimensions? Was he looping?

"Sam!"

"Just make sure they scan his head before he goes home."

The Lights Flickered

TOP down on a warm December night, she was a thing of beauty. Soft yet firm, giddy in sixth gear, she belonged in perpetual motion. The roadster purred as she pushed past eighty. It was a straight shot on the expressway for another twenty-six miles. Time for Sam to finalize his game plan.

"Straight-up poker won't work. Within fifteen minutes, they'll never call my raise again. I'll earn so little it won't even pay for a cafeteria lunch.

"Sure poker is about math. You have to know your odds of winning any given hand. Think of math as providing a framework, a guideline. It's like a coloring book. It helps you stay within the lines, but it doesn't dictate what color chips you use or how hard you press. Your stack, your table image, even your mood will tweak the poker knobs to tune in the best strategy.

"Strategy isn't static; it's a living thing. And it's a happy thing when you feed it a pot or two every orbit.

"It's also about reading your opponents. Just like you shouldn't call the tight guy's raise, you absolutely must raise the loose player's bet. If someone is betting many hands, they're taking lots of chances; they're not getting premium cards every hand. So the A-10 you absolutely would fold when up against the tight guy you now need to raise against the loose goose."

Sam pulled into the parking garage. He'd join a game in about ten minutes. What strategy would he start with tonight? He admired the old switcheroo: masquerade as a loose player … then, when every raise gets called, switch to tight-aggressive and clean up. He'd play cheap unraised hands, small suited connectors in late position, and stupid cards like 7-2, hoping to get lucky and hit the flop.

Sam arrived on the casino floor just after midnight. He passed the poker room without checking the list of active games. He wasn't ready. He needed to stretch his legs before sitting again, before staring down that fishing hole. While poker isn't a game of chance, it can be one of patience. You have to wait for an unbelievably fortunate combination of cards to hit the flop.

He used the last of his singles to get a bottle of water from a vending machine.

"Two sips and that's it," he told himself. Better to go thirsty than miss two or three hands for a bathroom break. No respectable ice fisher leaves the ice. Same for poker. What if one of those lost hands turned out to be a big pair? Anyone happily pisses on 7-2, but no one, no one shits on pocket aces.

"There's the restroom." Sam made a mental note of which way to turn when exiting the poker room.

"Whoa!" His eyes grew big as a trio of women brushed by. A buzz of adrenaline sparked cheek to cheek. Every beep and ding, every shout and siren fed that high.

Sam marveled at all the people dressed for success. It was working. Many of them were up big. You could see it on their faces and on the faces of those around them. The smiles at that craps table could stretch round the world.

"Just like an open bar at a celebrity wedding." Both success and free alcohol have supernova gravity. Put them together and—

"Boom!"

"Seven-out!" the stickman cried. A thousand eyes marked Sam for life. Fair enough. His outburst lost fortunes. Those cursed dice and maybe Sam himself would spend some time in the freezer.

It seemed two lifetimes before the cuckoo cried 10:00 a.m.

"Ace-something," he thought as he closed his eyes.

"Sir, it's on you." The dealer startled Sam.

"Call." Sam stacked two chips in front of him. He hoped they were the right color.

The flop came and went. He must have checked.

"Sir?"

Sam peaked at his cards and called.

"It's fifty, not fifteen."

Sam blushed. He needed to cash out and get something to eat. "What time is it?"

"Fifty to call."

"Is breakfast open at fifty to call?"

The dealer said nothing but his eyes shot darts at Sam.

"I raise."

Sam pushed a stack forward. It was probably a hundred.

His raise surprised the table. Was he only pretending to sleep? Isn't he the jerk who yelled "boom" last night?

The guy with two pair studied Sam, then his cards, then Sam again before calling.

The river was a nine.

The guy who used to have two pair now had a full house. "All-in."

Sam called in a heartbeat.

"Quad nines take the hand," the dealer announced, shaking his head.

Sam racked his chips and offered good luck to the players.

"Seat open, table 17."

Sam checked his watch. The tournament started at eleven: less than an hour to eat. The line for an egg sandwich stretched twenty minutes. It didn't matter. He could close his eyes for thirty seconds at a time. As he finished eating, he felt a pang of guilt. Had he tipped the dealer for that last win? He headed back to the poker room to sign up for the tournament. It was a safe thing to do. He would not rebuy. He hoped to play all afternoon without risking another penny.

Sam played tight for the first two hours, refusing to call any big bet unless he had a made hand. The next hour went much the same, except he semi-bluffed his flush on the flop and had no takers. His tight image gave him that win.

Sam yawned for nearly an hour. He sometimes folded without looking at his cards. The guy to his right had to wake him twice.

It wasn't much longer before the blinds got out of control. Sam's stack had less than five big blinds. If he continued to fold, he'd be lucky to survive until the next break.

What were his cards? K-4. Crap. Oh well, time to shower and get some sleep.

A guy in middle position raised. Sam could cover the raise but not much more. There were three players to act ahead of Sam.

Fold.

Call.

Fold.

The raiser might have a hand like A-K, A-Q, or some big pair. Sam's K-4 would be dominated. Calling made little sense. He should fold.

"All-in," I said dramatically, mocking the size of my own stack.

The raiser also pushed all his chips forward, isolating the third player who gladly folded.

"Two players."

The raiser showed his jacks. I started to reveal my hand but stopped when the flop hit without a king or four.

The raiser smirked. I would have said something witty, but my mind wanted only sleep.

King on the turn.

Time seemed to stop. The expected rush of adrenaline never came. I wondered if any of the folded hands had a jack. I knew eight cards, our two hands and the four cards on the board. Fifty-two minus eight ... forty-four cards, only two would beat me.

I heard laughter before my eyes recognized the queen of clubs. I won?

Maybe math too had a long night and decided to take the afternoon off. After that showdown, odds meant nothing. I won every hand until we drew for seats for the final table. Lucky? Maybe. But one thing for certain: I gave no tells. My brain-dead body had nothing to say. My strategy boiled down to two things: fold crap; raise a good hand enough to discourage drawing hands but not so much as to keep middle pairs from wanting to see the flop. My pairs held-up; my A-K hands caught. Heads-up, I raised every hand. Whenever my opponent called, I had a bigger hand.

When I dream about poker, I always raise my K-4.

The fluorescent lights made the room bright but not warm. Wendy reached for a blanket. The extra weight woke Adam.

"Where am I?"

"You're here with me."

Adam's eyes looked desperate. "I … I think I sold our kids."

"Don't be silly. They're on their way here now. I brought you a present."

"What is it?"

"It's big and red."

"Honey, I'm really not in the mood."

Wendy shook her head. "It's a fresh Fuji apple to bake into yesterday's pie."

Adam looked confused.

"Or you can eat it."

Adam smiled as he drifted back to sleep.

The joy on Adam's face was a gift.

"You better be dreaming about me."

"Wen?"

"Yes, Adam."

"Did you hear? I caught the straight flush on the river!"

"Adam."

"All diamonds. All the way to the ace."

"Adam, that's Sam's story."

"Nonsense, machines don't have stories."

"Don't play around; you're scaring me."

"I'm not playing. Well, I was playing. After I hit the royal flush, I cashed out and headed straight for the bathroom."

"You don't remember him?"

"Remember who?" Adam made a face. "Remember whom? I never could tell who's a who and whom's a whom."

"So you do remember?"

"Who?"

"First base," Wendy teased, holding back tears.

The buzz of the florescent lights distracted Adam. He suspected he might be dreaming. He pinched himself. It hurt way more than he thought it would.

"Sam," Wendy said gently, her mouth parched by heartache.

A far away look filled Adam's eyes. He didn't know anyone named Sam.

Wendy's hand trembled as she wiped a tear from her cheek. "Sam," she said as playfully as she could muster, "is the time traveller who helped you get to first base."

"Wen, you know I never played baseball. We couldn't afford—"

"Shut up and kiss me!"

Her lips were soft. Adam smiled. He remembered their first kiss.

Wendy reached for Adam's hand. "Finish your story."

Adam looked like he was in another world.

"Adam, about the poker hand, the straight—"

"Flush. Royal flush, actually. It's a rare bird. Getting a royal flush is like finding a lost friend."

"You just pick up where you left off."

"Never missing a beat."

Adam's hand felt cold.

"Adam, who told you about the royal flush?"

"No one told me. I hit the hand, cashed out, and pissed for like an hour—"

"Adam, I love you."

Adam's expression didn't change. He was rubbing his hands together, very slowly. He just needed to finish up in the restroom before he called to share his wonderful news. "Why is this water so cold?"

"Adam, your story has a name."

Adam wasn't surprised. Many things had names. The French had a different name for everything.

"What's the name of your story?"

It's like a whole nother language. Adam's laugh finished with a cough. Who told him that joke?

"Adam?"

"No, I'm Adam. Sam told me that."

A wave of relief rushed over Wendy's face.

"Wen, where's Sam?"

Grief returned to her lips. "He … he's lost."

"Lost? How could he be lost?"

"Do you remember when you jumped on Table *A*?"

Adam said nothing.

"Do you remember what happened?"

"I saw him a few days ago. He was heading to AC."

"You spoke with him?"

"Yes. Maybe. It's hard to keep everything straight. Sometimes I feel like I've been living two lives."

Wendy didn't speak. If she interrupted, he might shut down.

"I'm here with you now. I can feel it. But sometimes I'm far away on some cliff, staring into the mist for hours on end. I'm searching for something, something I might never find."

She squeezed his hand very tightly.

"Sam and I would wrestle for first pick." Adam smiled. "He hated being Phoebe, so he'd pretend to be a pony, you know, the one with its hooves in the air."

She pulled his hand to her chest. Pain nearly smothered her flame.

"Tell him…." Adam's voice crumbled deep in his throat. "Tell him he can be—"

His eyes softened. His breathing slowed.

Her light flickered in and out.

The room grew cold.

Love

We must live with what we have,
even when we have nothing.

Osaka by E. C. Flickinger
Dōtonbori, Osaka, Japan, circa 1990.

Sam 2.0

LEAVES rustled over a small patch of green as songs of swallows praised first light. Anxious plovers pranced upon still cold earth. Wings were tested for another day's journey or perhaps to signal the gathering of necessary materials. Homes were needed on high sheltered branches and deep in foreboding thickets.

The ancient fountain spat and sputtered, splashing icy water on a sleeping giant. He stirred but did not wake.

The wind shifted. An odd smell startled the birds.

"Pyuoo!" the alarm cried. The sky turned black as the birds took flight.

Sam lifted his chin. "Is that rain?"

He raised his hands to touch the drops. The sky brightened. The wind fell silent. The birds circled and swooped one last time before settling down to the tasks at hand.

Sam could hear their song. What were they saying with such lyrical calls, such rhythmic replies? Sam's face glowed as he absorbed the honeyed echoes.

"Was that love?" Sam laughed. "Or pleas for crawling delicacies or certain size twigs?"

A splash whispered something.

"Maybe the birds were encouraging each other to finish up and hurry home."

Home. So much meaning in a single word.

Sam surveyed the horizon. Where was his home?

"Who can see anything with all these feathers?" Sam puffed to blow a feather from his lips. There were many more birds here now than just minutes ago. They surrounded the fountain—not much green left on the ground or in the trees.

"Déjà vu." Had he been here before? No, not that he remembered. Yet something felt oddly familiar. He closed his eyes and brushed his finger tips along the blades of grass. Strength returned to his body. He was on his knees, then his feet. He stumbled for a few steps before stopping to look left and right.

"Which way is out?"

A stone path! He inched along, sometimes limping, sometimes crawling. He spotted an unusual tree in the distance. He ran a few steps before hobbling again. The tree still seemed so far away. When he stopped to rub his aching legs, the last ounce of energy drained from him as if his plug had been yanked from the wall.

He fell on his face.

"Ow," Sam whined as he smeared blood across his upper lip and onto his cheek. Then he saw it, just a few inches off the ground: a bird, perched on a small piece of damp wood, staring at him.

"Uh, nice birdy," Sam muttered as a peace offering. The bird's gaze remained fixed, daring Sam to blink first. Beads of sweat soaked Sam's brow. His eyes were so heavy. He would die here, alone, a victim of bird-rage.

A call from across the field broke death's silence. The standoff collapsed as the bird found her wings.

"Not funny," Sam moaned as he recognized the wood scrap as a small warning sign. Something was definitely not allowed in this place.

Sam rose to his feet, turning to see how far he had come. The juxtaposition of time and texture intrigued him: the ancient fountain adorned with wildflowers, the soft white petals against the hard gray stone.

He returned to the small patch of green, walking easier now. He ran his hand along the top of the fountain. It was smooth, polished by time. The walls of the fountain must have been carved from a single boulder. His lips parted in awe as he touched the Cosmos and Chrysanthemum.

"Also known as Kosumosu and Kiku."

How did he know their Japanese names?

Along a dark street still wet from rain, a slick patch caught Sam's eye. The glimmer had no color, only shades of gray. Sam closed his eyes. He needed to sleep, to dream about proper puddles with proper colors.

A fault in the matrix? He searched the trees, the signs, the lights—nothing was green or blue, red or yellow. How could this world breathe in black and white? Could it be the hour? Some moment in time when color wells waited to be filled?

What time was it anyway? Four a.m. on a Wednesday? Was it Wednesday?

"I've been walking for at least a minute. I should have reached the corner by now."

He was still squarely in front of the same lifeless building. He looked down at his feet. They were moving, but each step seemed to cover less and less ground.

He stopped to pick up a small stick before sitting. He rubbed the end against the curb. He yawned and yawned until he noticed a pattern emerging from his markings. Though he didn't recognize the symbols, he was sure they meant something.

Sleep tugged at his sleeve. He gave in and rolled onto his side, resting his head on the cold wet concrete.

He sometimes saw her face when he slept. Her lips were full and so very, very soft.

Six months later ...

Despite the instructions in Adam's will, a service was held in his honor in the lab. Only those who knew of Sam's predicament were invited. Addy established a window into Sam's world.

Sam looked awful, his hair on end, his T-shirt wrinkled. At least his boxers were black.

Wendy welcomed everyone with a few kind words. Addy wanted to cry but the background music soothed her.

"What's that song?"

"Something Adam wrote. An instrumental with a difficult name: twenty-something something. He built world-killing machines but couldn't write lyrics to save his soul."

"He nearly built a time travel device, not a—"

"It's okay, Addy, in another week or two, we would have…." Sam's voice faded off.

Wendy bowed her head. She swayed ever so slightly.

"I'm going to kill you, dear husband, for making me go through this." She turned to Addy. "We should have told the children. They should be here." The music changed to something more traditional. Wendy's eyes softened. She cradled a rose as if it were a baby.

Addy traced Wendy's steps. Both women placed their flowers next to Adam's ashes.

Addy waited for Wendy's signal. Wendy nodded.

"Sam, we'll be back as soon as we can. I need to close our window before initiating the resurrection."

"Don't call it that!" Wendy shouted. "This contraption is no God and Adam was no savior."

"Didn't you love your husband?"

"Addy, one day you'll understand. You'll find your soulmate and have children and watch those beauties grow into incredible adults."

This wasn't Wendy.

"Then you'll feel a gnawing ache until you realize—"

"Until you realize what, Wendy? What?"

"That you need more God and less sex."

Addy shook her head.

"Talk to me again after the birth of your second child when your husband goes on and on about having a date night. That damn convertible tangled the fuck out of my hair."

"Ah, guys," Sam interrupted, "I'm still here."

Addy started to terminate—

"Can I say something before I go?" Addy nodded. "Adam was going through a rough patch and lamenting how women are either sunsets or sunrises. His mentor told him: A good woman's both."

"And?"

"And what?"

"Why did you tell that story?"

"'Cause we all need someone who will be there in the morning."

Both women looked confused. Did Sam just say something meaningful?

Addy was the first to break the silence. "Sam, go to the fountain as fast as you can." Addy terminated the connection to Sam's dimension.

"Why does Sam need to be at the fountain?"

"Do you want the long or short answer?"

"The short one."

"SAM is unreliable."

"What does Sam have to do with—"

"I mean the machine SAM. The machine might not send Adam to the intended destination." Addy reached for her cell phone.

"Addy, put that away."

"I need to tell SAM what to do."

"I'm not even sure we should be doing this."

"It's what Adam would want."

"Immortality?"

"No, Wen. It's not about immortality. It's about accomplishing something of historical value." Addy sighed. "It's a shame he won't remember anything from the last two years. Once resurrected—"

"Don't use that word."

"Once reconstituted or whatever, he won't have very long. Whatever took Adam will take Adam prime."

"And what about the consequences of our actions? How do I explain this new Adam to my children?"

"Wendy, Adam gave life to Sam. SAM can do the same for—"

"This insanity ends now!"

"No, please, if not for Adam, then for science."

"And if we succeed? What happens when everyone wants to be reconstituted? Won't immortality make our lives meaningless?"

"Wen—"

"Aren't clones just another form of slavery? Our children will be sent to war over and over again!"

"There's always a risk that technology will be misused."

"Humanity is flawed. History is full of mass destruction."

"We don't spend our lives in the shower even though the shampoo directions say wash, rinse, repeat."

"Don't make light of an ugly situation."

"Okay, we'll stop. We'll ignore how our power source could mean free power for everyone. We'll never use that power to build new and wonderful things."

"Like what?"

"Like space craft capable of finding new worlds."

"I don't believe in extraterrestrial life."

"Our planet won't last forever."

"It only has to last until The Rapture."

Addy took a deep and nearly non-judgmental breath. "So pick a different miracle. Oh, wait, we can't … our power source could be used as a weapon. Put a detonator on SAM's back and blow a hole through the center of the Earth."

"Adam doesn't need this invention to be remembered as a great man."

"A husband? A father? That's enough?"

"It should be."

"Wendy, you, more than anyone else, should understand."

"Understand what?"

"You believe in God, right?"

"I do."

"And what did God do? He created us in His image."

"Yes."

"He gave us life."

"And light."

"Okay, and light. So, we have to believe humans aren't destined for destruction. God wouldn't want that to be our fate."

"He wouldn't. But that doesn't mean Adam needs to get his fifteen minutes of fame by usurping God's power to create life."

"Well, 'Adam Driver, husband, father, died today' isn't front page news."

Pain etched Wendy's face. "I don't think I can love a copy."

"Don't think of him as a copy. He could be the man you once loved … it's like cheating without cheating."

"Love is more than sex."

"Maybe someday my body will accept that fact—but not yet."

"So, why not store a copy of your own twenty-something body? You could live forever."

"There are a million ways to market this. Let's bring Adam back first."

"So it's all about the money, Addy?"

"We could spin on this forever. The people who invent things reap the rewards. Money isn't the end goal. It's a cause and effect thing."

"That's too vague."

"We could redefine transportation with a teleportation device ... though the lunch lines in Paris might get unmanageable."

Wendy wasn't buying it.

"Or we could fight obesity."

"So people could eat French food everyday and still lose weight?"

"Yes!"

"Sounds too good to be true."

Addy woke her phone, took a deep breath, then hit send. A series of command strings displayed on SAM's console ending with transfer -file Adam.app -to TableB -mod !Sam.specific.

"Addy, no modifications!"

"We have to!"

"Why do we need to remove all traces of Sam?"

"I can't love two men."

"Oh my God! I think I'm going to faint."

Adam's body began to materialize on Table *B*. He looked much younger and so much more attractive. He had gained more than a few stone in his last two years.

"Maybe I could love two men."

"Addy!"

"There was something irresistible about Adam."

"Irresistible? Adam?"

"He was selfless."

"He was obsessed with his career. It strangled our lives."

"All he wanted was to help Sam."

"Yes, that's what the world needs, another boy who doesn't wear pants to funerals."

SAM made a loud thump. SAM wasn't supposed to make loud thumps.

Adam flickered in and out. The wonder in his eyes morphed to fear.

Shhhhikt!

He was gone.

Addy panicked. She didn't know how to validate the destination: table B, the hotel room, the fountain? Maybe it took more power to get to the fountain. She reached for the little red button.

"Addy, wait!"

Sam? She didn't understand. How did a window open at the fountain? "Sam, is he with you?"

"Something's wrong." Sam fell to his knees. He put his hands to his ears. "Make it stop!" The whistling was maddening.

"Wendy, what should I do? What should I do?"

Wendy bent over at the waist. Her words were useless. Nothing she could say would stop her story from reaching its final page.

Drawing God

ADDY stood in front of a blank white board. "Any ideas?"

Wendy shook her head.

Guilt strangled Addy's face. "I … I might have entered the wrong shutoff for stage two."

Wendy's lips quivered.

"I'm sorry, Wen."

Wendy looked away. "We all make mistakes."

"But my mistake might have killed Sam."

"Right—"

Addy gasped.

"I mean some combination of errors may have—"

Addy waled as she rubbed her eyes raw.

"Addy, I have to tell you something. I … I tweaked the field stability." Addy's tears stopped. "And polished the diamond."

"Wendy! How could you? You might have killed Sam!"

"You told him to go to the fountain!"

The women stared at each other as they circled to gain position. One of them had a knife behind her back.

Laughter erupted.

"Addy, he might not be dead."

Addy's eyes lit up.

"If the energy surge bounced off the water—"

"We only shocked him?"

"Right. If the straw—"

"You mean flute."

"We have to check everything."

"Every line of code, every circuit down to the ground wires."

Addy fixed a loose connection. Wendy ran the functional test.

"Passed!"

"We're done?"

"Addy, we did it!" Addy looked anxious. "Go ahead. Dial Sam."

Addy bridged their two worlds. "There he is! Sam, can you hear us?"

The interdimensional link sparked and sputtered. Sam pushed himself to his knees. There wasn't much time left.

"Push the red button!"

No one responded.

"Addy! Push, the, little, red, button!"

"I can't, Sam. Anything could happen."

"In four." Sam began to crawl toward the portal. "One, two…."

"Sam?"

"Three."

"Sam!"

"Four!"

Addy slammed her fist against the big red button. The portal burned brilliant purple, shooting white-hot flares in all directions.

Shhhhikt!

As the smoke cleared, something, no, someone was standing tall in the center of the lab.

"Home at last! Addy, what happened to your nose?"

It wasn't the homecoming Sam expected. Wendy hugged him only once. Addy left in a huff. Was he to sleep in the lab?

He grabbed pen and paper, and headed outside. If he was destined to spend another night alone, he would sleep under the stars.

"And the tape…."

The door was locked. He walked down the stairs and looked around. Pennsylvania was nothing like Japan.

He sat on the bottom step, tapping his fingers as he studied a blank sheet of paper.

"Without the tape…."

He tore a strip about two inches from the right side, stopping
before he reached the bottom edge. He turned the sheet, ripped
another two inches, then turned the sheet again. He smiled at the
continuous path of paper.

What should he get first? Fruit? "Maybe a Japanese sports drink?"

It was a long evening. He fell asleep before the June sun set. His
body was still functioning on a December-in-Japan timezone.

Sam lurked in the shadow of the staircase as Addy pulled into the
parking lot.

Her top was off—down. The top of her convertible was down.

"Hi." Sam swallowed. "Hi, Addy!"

"Put that back in your pants." She pulled at the long slip waving
from Sam's pocket before bounding up the steps. As the door closed,
her face turned bright red. She desperately wanted to take it back,
but it was too late.

Sam's crooked smile decorated the laboratory entrance.

When he finally went inside, his two favorite people were
entrenched. Wendy was working with a bigger than usual wrench.
Addy was eating.

"Hey, hope you saved some for me."

Addy's eyes caught fire as she swallowed the last bite of breakfast.
She looked through Sam, ready to spit flames.

"Whatever, dude."

She watched for his reaction but took care to not break character.
She didn't want him to know her anger had already faded. At twenty-
six, she was at great risk of outgrowing her inner bitch. She laughed.
If she had stuck with acting, she'd only appear in fleeting scenes. No
one could stand ninety minutes of her badass persona, though she
could play the hell out of a red dress.

Leading roles were better left to ninnies. Even antiheroes need
some redeeming quality to be believable. Addy shut her eyes and
took a deep breath. For this scene, she would pull out all the stops.
She could see it so clearly … fifth grade home room when that girl
dared look at her Tommy.

Sam sat down. Addy was finishing her coffee. He squirmed a bit before looking across the table.

"I need a car."

"What kind of car?"

"Something sexy. I remember driving a roadster—"

"It was totaled," Wendy interrupted. How did she hear him from across the lab?

"Sorry!"

"It wasn't your fault."

"Right, it wasn't my fault. I knew that." After a long awkward pause, Sam cleared his throat. "Hey, Wendy, where were you—"

"I stopped at the high school to gossip about science."

"Oh right, the STEM lecture. I've always admired your teaching young women—"

"You are such an opportunist." Addy's face burned with anger.

Sam didn't defend himself. Addy got up to leave the table. Sam reached for her hand. Addy pulled away and stormed from the break room, clicking her heels deliberately with every step.

Sam's mind raced. He needed a way out of this mess. Just once he wanted to be the one who said something thought-provoking. The longer he lived in this little patch of poison, the more certain he became. The only way to win was to not play. He would take his ball and go home.

Emptiness drenched his soul. He didn't feel much like singing in the rain. He couldn't move his lips without enticing someone's wrath. Everyone conspired with the gods or the damn playwrights to keep his parts small. Maybe he was born too late, maybe too soon.

He reached for the newspaper. He would just read, if he could get his eyes to focus. He was a beast without a beauty, a scarecrow without a brain....

No. He was Sam and would push on despite the many pointy stones along his yellow brick road. "I'm the Tin Man, post-Oz," he thought as he raised the paper. He didn't want anyone to see the disappointment on his face.

Addy returned for a second cup of coffee. Sam smiled as he waited to catch her eye.

"What's that?" he asked, pointing at a rectangular carton. Adorned with a red bow, it looked important yet somehow misplaced as if it had been delivered to the wrong table.

"Truffles." She sat across from Sam. Her eyes were locked, swimming in his weepy gander.

"Truffles? In a box? On our table?"

"You sound like you're quoting a children's book." Sam didn't respond. He was still staring at the box of truffles. "Try one. Wendy won't mind."

"I'm pretty sure I wouldn't eat those even with green eggs and ham."

"You don't know what you're missing." Addy reached for the box.

"No, really, I'm a regular at the miss-out-on-everything club. And I promised Adam I wouldn't touch Wendy's stuff, though there is something 'acute' about her."

Addy pushed herself up from the table. "Do you flirt with everyone?"

"I'm not flirting. I wouldn't."

Addy sat back down. She watched Sam for signs of a tell.

"Look, Addy, I didn't even know Wendy had a pig."

"What?"

"Or a dog … whatever hunts truffles these days." Sam made a sour face. "I hate that word. Truffles. Yuk."

"Are you done?"

"I was done long before I even started. Wait."

"Truffles are candy."

"Get outta town."

"But they don't cost anything like the best fungi."

Sam leaned forward. "How much?"

Addy brushed Sam's hair from his forehead. "Two thousand a pound."

Sam's eyes got big. "Two grand? For pig snot? What a waste of a serious stack—"

"You play poker?"

"Why else would they call me Sammy Diamonds?"

"'Cause you … I got nothin'."

"'I hit the royal flush and took down a cool pound and a half.'"

"Pound and a half?"

"Of truffles, or the equivalent." He turned his head before whispering. "The pot was nearly three grand."

"That's not what I heard."

"Shh."

"That's not what I heard. Why are we whispering?"

"I don't like to brag."

"But you are a braggart—and a thief! Wendy told me that Adam shared that story on his death bed."

Sam covered his ears. "Don't say Adam and death bed in the same sentence."

"It's Sam's story, not Adam's," Wendy called from across the lab.

"Oh, Sam. I'm so sorry—"

"Too late." He lowered his head. "Now my nut flush will always remind me of—"

"Sam, forgive me." She touched his face. There was something wonderfully genuine in his expression. She had seen that same pain in her own eyes. "We can mourn him together."

"I'd like that." He pushed out his lower lip.

Addy laughed and returned a smile.

"Hey, look," Sam began tentatively, "I'm gonna head out to the grocery store in a bit. You need anything?"

"Some ice. Sometimes the coffee is too—" Addy stopped cold. "Sam, what's wrong?" Sam didn't answer. "Wendy, what's wrong with Sam?"

"He's afraid of ice," Wendy shouted from across the lab.

Addy shook her head. Both women returned to work, one tightened bolts while the other tweaked algorithms.

"I am not afraid of ice," Sam mumbled as he added "bag for Addy" to his grocery list.

The ceramic floor wasn't the best stage in the world but it would do. Destiny couldn't always choose its venue.

Sam peered into the bathroom mirror. He was ready. He would be that microphone.

"How's everyone tonight? I'd ask where you're from, but I don't care."

Sam pretended to cower from an angry audience.

"Look, I'm old-fashioned. I grew up on the playground without parental guidance … survived childhood without streaming video. Hell, I even believe in the Oxford comma."

A few centenarians whooped their approval.

"A big thank you to those old farts. Remember them—they'll be the ones blocking the exits after the show."

The audience stared indignantly.

"Hey, I'm not prejudiced … no matter what that internet says."

Sam took a deep breath.

"For all I know I'm related to one or more of you black folks." Sam pointed. "Or you Jews." He pointed again. "Maybe both. I wouldn't mind being rich … and beautiful."

Sam looked down for four awkward seconds. He was surprised to hear boos at the end of that joke.

"I apologize, but the sign out front did say something about comedy."

Apology not accepted. Guess the rich know they're rich and the beautiful know—

"People have made fortunes suppressing minorities. But that's ancient history, right?"

The crowd cheered. Sam shook his head. Why do the masses equate historical contempt with current day virtue?

"History is embarrassing, isn't it? Take what's-his-name, the father of our country—yeah, I know—all he did was cross the Delaware and free a nation. But he owned slaves, 127 slaves to be exact. Unbelievable, right? So really, we should hate that dude. *Wir sollten diesen Typen hassen.*"

The crowd fell eerily silent. Maybe that German joke was a bit too pointed.

"Well, we've covered war, slavery, my stupidity…. What's left? Oh! Religion." Sam smiled. "Isn't having a religious spouse a good thing?" He paused to let the setup simmer.

"Take my wife … please." Sam laughed … alone. Not many Henny fans out there. "Every time I disappoint her, she can pray for someone better."

Yes, that was a clap from the audience. Not quite the momentum Sam had expected.

"Well, I don't sin any more than I have to." Sam scanned the audience. No one was on their feet; no one was awake. "So when someone asked me to pick a side, I thought she meant good versus evil. Was I wrong! The issue was political correctness versus legalizing marijuana."

Sam raised and lowered his outstretched arms, weighing the pros and cons on an imaginary scale of justice.

"I offered to flip a coin—either choice would mask the truth."

Sam cringed.

"Wrong move. We started fighting about immigration, gerrymandering, all kinds of serious shit. I should have just said no. It worked for drugs."

The crowd turned on Sam.

"Come on, it was funny … my wife laughs at me all the time."

Nice recovery.

"They say youth is wasted on the young. I get it, but it isn't easy being young without the benefit of our years of experience. Experience gives us perspective."

Sam nodded as he extended an open hand to the young beauties in the front row.

"Youth is intoxicating."

Women under thirty applauded.

"Millennials are cool, right? Well, not cool like that word meant when we were in our twenties. It's now more socially acceptable to live with your mother then it is to find work … or have sex."

A hush blanketed the auditorium.

"What else is cool?"

"Not you." The heckler nearly brought the house down.

"Jazz." Sam's eyes widened. "It's living on instinct. You push here, pull there, never one hundred percent sure you'll find your way home."

Something in Sam's expression endeared the audience.

"Jazz is pure. Everything else makes you wait. And you don't want to wait for someone to score your whole life before you play your first note."

Sam paused for an eight count. It felt right.

"My advice … don't wait for anyone or anything."

A toilet flushed. An older gent with half an unlit stogie emerged from stall three.

"Not bad, brother, not bad at all. But check your history book. I'm pretty sure if we had lost that war we'd still be speaking English." He winked as he tapped his newspaper against the top of the counter and turned to leave.

"Sir, do you happen to have another cigar?"

"Yes, I do," the gentleman acknowledged on his way out.

Sam emerged from the restroom. "I told you the German joke wouldn't cut it. And now I'm addicted to graffiti."

"I didn't look."

"Not even on the stall's walls?"

"No, but I'm pleased to hear you use internal rhyme."

"Damn poets."

"Seriously Sam, are you ok? You were in there a long time."

"I wash my hands before and after."

"So do I!"

Sam shook his head. "I was taking my shot, gambling my soul."

"A gambling soul risks all / to wake / in the arms of a stranger."

"Did you just make that up?"

"Nah, it's the kind of shit that filled my head twenty years ago."

"Did you try using drops and turning your head to the side?"

"Here's another one. When a man reaches middle age / he becomes / a teenager again—"

"Only this time / he has money."

"Do you have to finish all my lines?"

"I doubt it was ever yours. You probably appropriated it."

"You're a … a … paperback comedian!"

"Take that back! Adam, take it back!"

"Sam, your contribution was a condom."

"Don't be so literal. Sometimes I help out a friend, but that's not my biggest contribution."

"No? Then what?"

"It's a toss up between issue resolution and technology purveyance. Maybe marketing consultation."

"What kind of marketing advice?"

"You know, things to make the hard science more fluffy."

"Name a furry thing."

"Fluffy, not furry. Honestly, Adam, you'd be lost without me."

"Name a fluffy thing."

"Okay, the branding for the divide-by-zero technology."

"So 'big red button' is your claim to fame?"

"In part. There's also the flute."

"The flute?"

"Remember when we were in that bar and you used a straw to represent the energy/matter power flow?"

"You mean when I asked for a straw and everyone looked at me like I was an insensitive ass, someone who cared nothing for the planet's well-being?"

"Well, you were drinking beer. No one drinks beer through a straw, especially not a *Hefeweizen*."

Adam's face went blank. He was not the insensitive ass who cared nothing for the well-being of the planet; nor was he the fool who drank beer through a straw. He was a true scientist who used real straws to demonstrate real energy/matter analogies in real bars. Adam half-smiled. Maybe his life wasn't as tragic as it felt.

"Adam, are you even listening to me?"

"You were saying something about needing holes."

Sam instinctively paused for the laugh track. Nothing. "You realized we needed holes in the straw—to allow the excess power to escape—so I asked if your so-called straw was plastic or metal and you said it was a hybrid force field reinforced metal." Sam paused for dramatic effect.

"So?"

"So a metal straw with holes isn't a very useful straw. Ask any kid, three or older, and they'll tell you the same: not a straw. A metal tube with holes is a flute."

"OK, I've got it now. Your contribution was putting a condom on a flute."

"Don't call my baby ugly!"

Adam wondered what happened to that straw. Did he take it with him? Did it end up in a landfill? Was he an insensitive ass after all?

"I'm very proud to be the first to introduce a magic flute in a fictional or non-fictional story."

"Hold up on your acceptance speech. It's not true."

"Maybe not in this timeline."

Adam laughed. Why did he feel nothing in one moment and everything in the next?

"Don't laugh at me."

"I'm not. I'm laughing with you."

"You know I can tell when you are lying, right?"

"And you know that I know you," Adam paused to catch his breath, "substituted a ribbed condom for our approved membrane."

"I have no knowledge of any blasting of any walls. I'm pretty sure I was in Japan when that allegedly happened."

"Sam, come clean or I'll—"

"I'm sorry."

"What? Say that again, a little louder." Adam pinched both ends of an imaginary string and pulled those ends farther and farther apart.

"I apologize to you and to the scientific method. I'm sorry for unnecessarily changing an irrelevant variable."

Adam clenched his teeth. "And?"

"And I apologize to the wall."

Adam looked at Sam cross-eyed.

"I'm sorry I risked our lives."

Sam placed the bag of ice on the break table. "I hope you melt."

He turned to watch Addy as she worked high on a ladder.

"Come here," he mouthed to her.

She shook her head.

Sam pulled out a drawing tablet and a *6B* pencil, contraband from Adam's art supplies. He smiled when he caught Addy checking him out.

She smiled back, giggling as she stretched her neck to confirm Wendy was absorbed in her work.

"Whatcha doin'?" she asked.

"Nothin'."

"You're obviously not doing nothin'."

"Obviously."

"So you lied."

"I never lie." The right corner of Sam's mouth curled ever so slightly.

Ah, his tell. "You just lied again."

Sam loved Addy for her playfulness, not just because she was the most beautiful woman on the Eastern Seaboard. He hadn't seen every state, not even Alaska or Hawaii.

"Addy, have you been to Hawaii?"

"Not yet. Why?"

"I'd love to make it to those islands one day."

Addy bit her lower lip. What was he getting at? Sam didn't do small talk. Was he trying to—she noticed a piece of lettuce on his shoulder.

"Sam, did you have a salad for lunch?"

"I don't eat salads … and it's way too early for lunch."

"Liar, liar. That was Wendy's lunch. Food in the fridge isn't common property."

"Well, whoever ate that salad probably didn't see a name marked on the box."

"Wendy's lunch goes on the right side of the top shelf, Adam's on the left—"

Sam looked dejected.

"Sorry, Sam."

"And your lunch goes in the middle?"

"Yes."

"So, you went between them?"

Addy squared her shoulders. "Every day."

"I saw no leftover chili in the middle of the top shelf."

"I ate my lunch while you were at the grocery store."

"Maybe you murdered the salad in the break room with the knife, Miss Mustard."

"It was a Caesar salad."

"No wonder you stabbed him."

Addy laughed. "Et tu, Brute?"

"I've never been to Rome."

"Me either."

"You should go. That is, if you want to."

"I do."

"I do, too ... wait, did we just get married?"

Addy blushed. So he was floating possible honeymoon locations after all.

"So, Addy?

"Yes, Sam."

Sam's eyes sparkled. She said yes. "How did you know I had salad for second breakfast?"

"There's a clue on your shoulder, Samwise."

Sam brushed his shoulder, then scratched a few short lines.

"What are you working on?"

"Some project. Hoping to finish it before the weekend; could use the moolah."

"What project?"

"An illustration for a children's book."

"Let me see your precious."

Sam blocked her view with his shoulder. "You're into *The Lord of the Rings*?"

"Duh, but don't change the subject." She maneuvered back and forth. "Show me your stuff."

Sam blushed as Addy stood up to peer over his defenses.

"Cheater."

"Is that God?"

"I'm not worthy of The Almighty but the money was too sweet to pass up."

Addy watched Sam's hand lightly stroke the paper.

"Addy, how do you feel about the Commandments?"

"The Commandments?"

"Moses … coming down the mountain … stone tablets—you must have heard—"

"Of course I know about the Ten Commandments."

Sam wriggled his nose. "Would you break one?"

"Which one?"

"The second one."

She didn't respond.

"The one about graven images."

She didn't respond.

"Look, I'm not trying to trick you."

"You have to answer for yourself."

"Wow, did you just get metaphysical with me?"

Addy blushed. She looked good in that color. "A graven image is an idol. The Second Commandment tells us not to worship such false gods."

"An idol? Not a drawing?"

Addy held her breath, hoping that would keep her from giggling.

"So it's okay if I draw God?"

"Yes."

"For money?"

"Yes, you can't steal lunches from the fridge forever."

Sam sighed. He had other plans for that paycheck.

"So, Sam, what's your inspiration for your depiction of God?"

"Can I explain by telling you a story?"

"As long as it's not about bananas."

"I don't tell stories about bananas. That was Adam's thing."

"Sorry, Sam, I don't mean to keep—"

"It's okay." Sam took a deep breath. "I didn't watch much TV as a kid. But when my friends were busy—"

"Both your friends?"

"Again, Adam's joke."

Addy looked down and bit her lip.

Sam took thirty seconds to compose himself. "I know it's hard for you, too … since I remind you of him."

Addy teared up.

Sam took her hand. "I literally can't get him out of my head."

She shifted in her seat.

"Addy, someday, when you look into my eyes, you won't see a great person and first-rate scientist; you'll see me."

"Sounds like a flubbed movie line."

"You saw that one? It ruined blue for me."

"Sam, can we get serious for a minute?"

Sam folded his hands in front of himself.

"What was your inspiration for your Almighty?"

"If I tell you, you'll laugh, maybe hit me."

"I won't laugh but I can't promise I won't hit you."

"Cross your heart and—"

Addy started to cross her heart.

"No! Stop! Don't do that. I won't be able to think for a week if you do that."

Addy smiled without blushing. She drew her fingers across her lips to zip them.

"No, that's no good either."

She had his full attention but asked again with her eyes.

"I'm sure there's a commandment against torture."

"Tell me."

"Captain Crush."

"Captain Crush?" She made a face.

"No, no, I meant Captain Kangaroo."

"I don't know a Mr. Kangaroo—"

"Captain, please. I'm pretty sure he earned his stripes."

"Sam, it's great that you're drawing." She winked. "I think Adam sketched, too."

"Okay, now you're pissing me off."

They mock-wrestled for a hundred heartbeats.

She combed her hand through her hair. "When you're finished with God, call me."

Sam's mouth opened wide.

"That didn't come out right."

And she was gone. The smartest, most playful, most beautiful woman in all the world was gone.

Sam clutched his chest. He couldn't breathe. Every molecule of oxygen followed her home.

Diamond in the Ruff

THE alarm rang for a second time. Addy didn't have the strength to silence her foe. When she finally sat up, she stared into space. The trophy mounted on her wall eventually caught her eye. She approached, bowing before lifting her old friend from the rack.

"Well, Maggie, we had a good run."

Addy traced Maggie's scars with her finger before dangling the water gun at her side. She practiced a few quick draws as she headed to the kitchen. With a boom and a bang, she hid her childhood behind the pots and pans.

Wednesday, 7:48 a.m. In only two minutes, the first bell would send the gathering mob to homeroom. Where was she? The support of a young collaborator would reinforce the importance of everyday math.

The bell.

To Wendy's surprise, the children seemed genuinely interested in the usefulness of division, especially the two girls in front. They were quite competitive.

"Next topic, temperature—"

The students oohed when Addy poked her head into the classroom and again as she maneuvered past the teacher's desk.

"All our gadgets use the Celsius scale. So when adjusting one of the temperature sensitive systems, like the emergency shutdown, we convert the required degrees Fahrenheit to the appropriate Celsius value. Addy, can you give us an example?"

Addy squared her shoulders. All hands went up.

Wendy motioned for the squirming to stop. "Everyone, this is Addy, one of our key scientists. Addy?"

"Sure. Thanks, Wen."

Wendy shook her head without realizing it. Why did everyone insist on calling her that? Two more letters was all she asked for … two more effing letters.

Addy seemed distracted by the sixty or so eyes locked on her.

"Eyes up … here." The class giggled as she pointed to her eyes. "Say we want to make a fifteen degree Fahrenheit change." She stepped to the left, sixty eyes followed. She stepped right—the first ten rows melted onto the floor.

"Addy, please pick a spot before you do some real damage."

More giggles.

"Sorry. To convert degrees Fahrenheit to degrees Celsius, we take the desired delta temperature minus thirty-two…. I screwed up."

Wendy's world erupted in giggles. She had to step in. No children would die on her watch. Some words weren't safe around teenagers. All children were lost in hormonal highs, arms raised, hands twisting and twisting as if screwing light bulbs.

Wendy spoke quickly. "All readings are in Celsius, so we take a Fahrenheit temperature and convert it to Celsius—and bing, bang, boom, science makes the world go round."

One person applauded from the farthest corner of the room. It was Sam. Wendy hadn't noticed him until he stood up.

"Ms. Wendy, I hope you don't mind my interrupting, but there are other interesting uses for everyday maths that I'd like to share with the class."

The class stopped twisting.

"Yes, maths. Everybody says there's a one in seventeen chance to catch a pocket pair pre-flop. Sounds mysterious but it's not. Look."

Sam pulled a deck of playing cards from his pocket.

"I need a volunteer." Most hands were still in the air. "How about you, young lady?"

The class oohed twice before giggling.

"Pick a card, any card."

Addy chose but didn't look. She handed her card to Sam.

"Very good." Sam showed Addy's card to the right, center, and left side of the class.

All students sat quietly with neatly folded arms. Even Billy, the eldest boy, seemed to be recovering. He would remember this day for the rest of—

"This ordinary deck started with fifty-two cards. After Ms. Addy selected the seven of hearts, we now have fifty-one cards in our deck. How many of those remaining fifty-one cards are sevens?"

All hands went up, except Billy's. He was picking his nose.

"Sorry, class. My question was for Ms. Addy."

"Three," Addy answered proudly.

"Right, three—your intelligence overshadows your beauty."

A chorus of eww's and aww's echoed from all four walls.

"So three of the remaining fifty-one cards will give us another seven. Three divided by fifty-one reduces to one over seventeen. So, on average, we'll get a pair every seventeen hands."

The classroom cheered.

"Of course, the best starting hand is a big pair!"

The bell called time. The students scurried out. Several stopped to leave an apple for Addy.

Wendy had her hands deep inside the chassis, tweaking a poorly performing subsystem. SAM was doing better but still not living up to expectations.

"So Wen, what part of STEM did you focus on this morning?"

"Sam, you were there. And please don't call me Wen."

"Sorry, I was distracted by your assistant."

Wendy turned to Addy who hadn't heard a word of conversation since she picked up her coffee.

"Addy?"

"Yes, Wen?"

"Throw out an idea, any idea."

"We could try an inverted—"

"That's what I'm talking about!"

Addy looked confused.

"And Sam, you come here too. We need this to be a threesome."

Sam smirked. When he stood up, his right foot was numb.

"On my way!" He took a step, shook his foot, took another step. "Addy, help! I'm stuck on rinse and repeat."

"OK, team, I'm going to ask questions and each of you will answer truthfully to the best of your ability. Got it?"

"I'm all for threesomes but maybe you women should handle this science polygraph yourselves."

Addy looked pale. "No, I'm out. You two can go at it. Sam can be the naive yang to Wendy's expert yin."

"Ready, Sam?"

"Well—"

"I'll ask you a series of questions; just say the first thing that pops into your mind. Then, after that round, we'll switch roles."

Addy smiled. "Sam, that's when you ask Wendy stupid questions to help her rethink her assumptions. Can you do that?"

"Seriously, you think I can't ask stupid questions?"

"Perfect. That's exactly what we're looking for! Guys, I have to go now, but I'll be back after I wake from this nightmare."

"So, Sam," Wendy began, "What color are your eyes?"

"Brown?"

"Sam, you have to answer confidently or this isn't going to work."

"Brown. I'm eighty percent certain they're brown. I'm an interdimensional traveler, not a mutant."

"Enough evasive tactics! Do you have a tack in your shoe?"

"Of course not."

Wendy smirked. He probably had a tack in both shoes. His eyes were definitely blue.

Sam looked at the ceiling. Why were so many women ogling him today? He swung his legs as far as possible from Wendy and casually checked his fly.

"Before we continue, why don't you tell me about the most significant event of your teenage years. You know, before I met Adam."

"It's hard to say. It's all a big fog to me."

"Focus!" Wendy cleared her throat. "Focus."

"Well, we ate and slept and ran like the dickens."

"OK, don't tell me if you don't want to."

"Wen, if you could ask a more specific question, that would really help."

"Tell me about the summer before Adam's senior year of high school."

"That spring, I remember wanting to escape. I was sick of high school and especially disillusioned with track. I wanted to get on with my life. I would have skipped my senior year altogether if I could have. So when that door opened, I just walked through."

"Door? What door? Were you always a traveler?"

"No. An opportunity landed in my lap, so I took it."

"A job? An inheritance? A woman?"

"No. Can we stay on track?"

"I'm asking the questions, buddy."

"Since I needed a break, I got my wisdom teeth pulled right away, rather than wait till summer. It took forever to heal. My gums bled every time I tried to run, even weeks after the surgery. Something was wrong. I tried to tough it out; I really did, but I lost my spark."

"You were like Samson, but with teeth."

"Is that a question?"

"You were like Samson, but with teeth?"

"Yes, well, without teeth."

Wendy nodded. She finally understood.

"Wendy, I wish I had met you that summer."

"Enough, back to work. Ask me your best stupid question."

Sam thought for several minutes. Wendy began to snore.

"Pink or blue?"

"Sorry, what?"

"We almost always have a choice, but sometimes we're afraid to face that decision."

"What are you saying?"

"Which pill would you pick: pink or blue?"

"Is this a gender-biased question?"

"No, this isn't about gender or race or about anything other than choice. And the fact you asked that question makes it hard for me to see you as anything other than a woman. Sure, an attractive woman, who's intelligent, brave, compassionate...."

Wendy sat quietly. She didn't want to interrupt.

"So, my friend, which will it be: pink or blue?"

"Blue."

"Blue?"

"Pink."

"You don't have to decide so quickly. You're making a life-changing decision, not choosing a snack."

"I'm not good at this kind of stuff. Do we have any crackers? My blood sugar's out of whack."

An odd mist danced in the corners of the lab.

"Was someone smoking?"

"Addy, you're back!"

"I'm here to save the day."

"Thank God. Wendy and I just can't sort these things without you."

"Shoot!"

"Would the targeting device be faster if we lent some of the booster's high-test fuel to the targeting device?"

"It might." Addy was surprised by Sam's intelligent question. "It would change the design to a parallel configuration as we'd be sharing both data and power. We'd have to add hundreds of more validation points."

"Is that a yes?"

"A qualified yes, but my new targeting design makes your question moot."

Both Wendy and Sam looked dumbfounded.

"Let me explain. Currently, the booster is available for only stage three, which makes sense since it takes more power to bend the timeline and transfer the subject than it does to select the correct timeline."

"I see her lips moving but her words make no sense."

"Providing additional power for the timeline selection might speed up that selection, but it's more about accuracy than speed."

"Accuracy. Right."

"It's not very helpful to find the wrong timeline a little faster."

"Isn't it nice how she's learned to speak gibberish so fluently?"

E. C. Flickinger

Wendy nodded. "She always was the smart one. No wonder Adam wanted to have her baby."

"Funny, guys. Have you ever wondered why Sam ended up in an alternate dimension?"

Sam opened his mouth to speak.

"Sam, don't answer a rhetorical question. Either stage two accessed the wrong dimension or the data transfer to stage three was somehow corrupted."

Sam licked his lips. "And that's a bad thing?"

"Two bad things, actually. It's highly unlikely we had a data error. So stage two's algorithm was the likely suspect. Till I rewrote it. Someday, it will be sold in the plumbing aisle along side the flux capacitor."

"Oh, I can spend hours in the plumbing aisle—"

"Men." Wendy and Addy shared a look.

"The new method reuses Adam's dimension separator but revamps the dimension selector. It even remembers the prior selection and revalidates it automatically."

"Automatically. Ow! I bit my tongue."

"Time can branch if something significant happens, like someone alters a key event or artifact."

"Well, the toilet isn't quite flushing right—"

"No, it would take more than TP tampering."

"You know, they're rationing toilet paper these days. Wait, you're not suggesting I used the bidet."

"Sam, if anything, I'm suggesting you eat less sugar."

"Enough about me. Let's hear more about your genius invention."

"So I asked myself, what assumption could we change to end this nightmare? Duh! I'd be the first to build a working time machine!"

"Totally agree. Months ago, I recommended we use elected presidents as key event factors."

"Slow down, Sam. You might hurt yourself."

"He wanted to use governors, but I said who cares about politics at the state level? Most versions of California would have elected Arnold, so it isn't a very good differentiator."

"Did I hear you correctly? You think you were the first to suggest using presidential history to identify timelines?"

"It was an obvious conclusion after everyone cried foul about the foolish electoral college. States' rights don't matter anymore."

"Sam, I thought you were a registered Republican."

"I am, but there aren't any laws about having to vote a straight-party ticket."

"So you didn't vote for him?"

"I'm not going to answer that question. I learned to dance before you were born."

Addy saw Sam's tell. "I bet you didn't even vote."

"I would have if I had been in town. And I so would have advised everyone to drop that "again" part. America has always been great. Adding "again" offended anyone who looks on Colonial America as a flawed experiment."

"Slavery of any kind is abhorrent."

"On this we agree."

"Good."

"Addy, sorry to say this, but did you graduate as an English major with a math minor?"

"There must be some residual timeline pollution or some kind of looping going on … or you are one very lucky guesser."

"Check the lab journal, Addy. It'll confirm what I'm saying … unless I traveled back in time and altered the log."

"It's my idea. It's already on my resumé. See?"

"Addy, I don't even know what cum laude means much less understand that summa part, so it stands to reason I wouldn't be the one to invent time travel."

"Okay, fine. Let's leave it at that. My new algorithm uses a subset of recently elected presidents to differentiate the timelines. It makes sense—who else would have voted in two brothers, an actor, and what's-his-name."

"You left one out."

"He would have been elected in far too many timelines."

"And Ronald wouldn't have?"

"Yes, of course he would, but Adam hardcoded him as P_0 in like a thousand places. It was—"

"Faster to just go with it."

"Weird. We're finishing each others sentences."

"So, Addy, what's your equation?"

"T' = P_0 + 2B + 45."

"No, you didn't."

"Didn't what?"

"You didn't reduce what's-his-name to a constant."

"So what if I did?" Addy stuck her nose in the air. "If my testing goes well, I will prove beyond a shadow of doubt that Adam's algorithm produces two answers, where my solution yields exactly one."

"Wow. One dimension, not two. The correct one?"

Addy made a face. "And as they say, the rest is left for the reader. Now I must head out for a few test harness components before we can get presidential."

Addy paused for comment but there was nothing more that could be said.

"Damn it!" Addy cried as she pulled on the vacuum-sealed door, wrenching her shoulder.

Wendy and Sam shouted in unison: "Push!"

The door slammed behind her.

When the alarm rang, Addy sat up, bright eyed and bushy tailed.

"What a weird dream! He was there; she was there—"

It was 6:30, not nearly eight.

"What's on the agenda this morning?"

She stretched.

"There aren't any trials today. Though I could rewrite that selection code."

She ran her hand through her hair.

"Oh, the STEM lecture's this morning."

She reached for the largest shirt she owned.

"This boy gets buttoned all the way up."

She pulled up her jeans, her fat jeans. Her curves disappeared.

"I wonder what Sam was up to last night."

Nightfall rolled in from the east, blanketing the suburbs. His heart raced. He wanted to shout "raise!" from the rooftops. He lowered his head as a strange sadness filled his heart. He still felt the loss of the Taj.

"Oh!" He smiled as he twisted in front of the mirror. He looked good in black, be it funeral or bank heist. He laughed. To become a true ninja, he needed only a sword or maybe some *shuriken*.

His eyes widened. "It could work." He'd sneak into the lab, pawn the diamond, and head to the nearest game. "Consider it a short-term loan."

The lab was eerily quiet.

"Where are you, my little precious?"

A sign hung above his namesake. SAM: Select, Acquire, Map. It was of little help. He would have to guess. Who could keep all this science in their heads?

"Stage three?"

Sam searched the stage three chassis. It was hard to see through the sea of wires.

"Oops!" Sam's fingers brushed a connection. "Must have been a weak solder joint to bust apart like that."

Worst of all, there was no diamond.

"Stage one or two?"

Can't be stage one. The select stage only sets the destination. Even science doesn't need a gem to pick "yesterday."

Sam tried the stage two door. The chassis wouldn't budge.

"Locked?" Of course it was locked. There's a huge diamond inside.

Sam pulled a credit card from his wallet. Even an over-extended card can defeat a cheap lock.

Sam tried twice but failed. He closed his eyes and envisioned the latch sliding ever so slightly.

"Voilà!"

The inside of the unit looked familiar.

"The diamond should be just on the other side of that elaborate pedestal."

Sam's hand probed every surface. Nothing.

"No, no, no!"

No poker tonight.

Sam shuffled into Adam's office, hoping to spot a stack of hundred dollar bills. He frowned as he rifled through the desk.

"Adam must have a secret or two that could be sold on the black market."

Black market. Why's it called that? Why is black a bad color?

Sam wrapped his hand round his chin. "So, if we were, say, watching a movie...." He fired his next words at Adam's chair: "Who's the villain?"

The leatherette seemed clueless.

"The guy in the black hat, that's who." Our words hold us hostage.

Sam pulled on the top drawer of the filing cabinet jammed in the corner of Adam's office. It contained one folder, marked top secret.

"Only Adam would mark something top secret and leave it in an unlocked cabinet."

Sam marveled at the folder's contents.

"Forget that time travel stuff. Adam's been hiding his true intention for years."

Adam the treasure hunter ... the thief.

"*Raikiri,* huh." If Sam couldn't borrow the diamond, he'd take this file. Adam owed him that much.

Wait a minute. Hadn't he recently declined an invitation from a friend of a friend?

"When is that party?"

Sam smiled as he knocked on the apartment door. He tested the numbers to see if they were loose. Maybe one of the numbers had spun around and changed the address. This probably wasn't the right place. He should go.

Both numbers were nailed tight. He knocked again.

"It's open." The woman at the door smiled awkwardly as if trying to place Sam's face.

"I'm Sam."

Knowing his name seemed enough to earn a nod and a welcoming flourish.

She stumbled backward as she waved him in. A kind young man caught her and pulled her to his chest. She might have twisted an ankle or spilled her drink if it weren't for the kindness of strangers.

"Oh."

The man was a stranger to Sam, not the host. She probably knew him, though she now seemed less grateful as he hadn't yet let go.

The room was filled with smoke. Most of the cigarettes were in the hands of women. It made no sense. Sure, women are the new men. He knew that. All men knew that. But why would such strength need the nostalgic glamor of smoke and ash?

Sam had lost track of where he was and began to look for landmarks. He smiled as he saw a couple exit the restroom. He pushed through countless warm bodies: male, female, other. Maybe gender didn't matter. He wasn't even sure how to address the woman hosting this party. Host? Hostess? She/her? Sam bit his lower lip. Language had moved on.

He leaned against the living room wall, staring into a crowd of nameless faces. Before the end of the night, he would put a name on a few of those faces.

"Maybe not the right names."

He laughed.

"Ooh, I'll call that one Bob."

After a drink or two, he might even be persuaded to tell a joke.

His flight instinct begged him to flee from this time trap. His eyes found the exit—

Someone tapped his shoulder.

"Hi, I'm—"

Sam smiled but he hadn't heard her name. The music was too loud.

He nodded as she spoke. He couldn't hear a word but the rhythm of her voice soothed him. Her lips opened and closed pleasantly, and she often smiled from the corner of her mouth. She might have been going on and on about solar panels, but she was attractive and drinking dark soda. Tonight that would be enough to forget raising top pair and put a hold on broadening his understanding of proper gender pronouns.

She giggled as she drank. Sam watched intently in case she choked.

His concern was in vain. She likely practiced giggling even when she wasn't at a party. It was a skill for sure.

"I'm Sam," he shouted. "Can I get you some ice?"

She shook her head as she reached for his hand. "Glad to meet you."

Sam wished she had repeated her name. Try, try, again—

"I'm Sam."

"Yes, I know. I think we've met before." She giggled.

"I'm a writer." He leaned forward. "I'm not afraid of ice."

She smiled. "A novelist?"

He nodded. "My current project is a trilogy of novellas."

"Trilogy of novellas," she repeated. "I like the sound of that." Yes, she did. She said it a second and a third time. There were definitely two if not four fingers of rum swimming in her lovely bubbles.

"I'm jotting down tons of notes," Sam added confidently.

She smiled and drank and giggled.

"Soon, I'll need a new ream."

Her giggle turned gurgle at the word ream. Her eyes seemed confused.

"When I'm in the shower—"

She spit rum—not a lot, not enough to end a friendship.

"Sorry, I didn't mean to do that."

"I know. Sometimes it drives me crazy and I just have to get it out."

Her posture changed. "Sorry, I just remembered I was looking for someone."

He grabbed her hand as she turned to leave.

She slapped him and stormed away. She would have tossed her drink in his face but it was gone. All her bubbles were gone.

Sam turned and nodded to another woman. She didn't nod back. The music stopped just as Sam spoke.

"Hi. I was born in another world."

"So I've heard."

The room erupted in laughter.

Sam started for the exit. The room was thick with smoke. He could barely see. He might have accidentally touched a person or two.

"Sam!"

"Sam!"

He didn't hear. He needed to forget his name. He opened the door and hurried home.

Locked and Loaded

ADDY returned to the lab unexpectedly. She had forgotten something or so she said. Sam watched her pretend to study a book in Adam's office. Why was that space still considered Adam's property? Shouldn't Wendy just paint over his name to claim that room as her own? Don't all new leaders need to take control, put their spin on everything? No, Wendy wasn't that kind of leader. She saw what needed to be done and did it without fanfare, though she didn't seem to enjoy it much, not anymore.

Maybe Wendy considered that office a kind of library where anyone could come and go. In a library, despair can't take the seat next to you.

Or maybe she needed a closet. The lab was rife with displaced mops.

Sam followed Addy into the dimly lit office, which now seemed more museum than anything else. The piles of books, the notes, the drawings—everything smelled of musty grass. It would soon prove hard to be in that room alone.

"Sam?"

Sam remembered. This room had been a closet. When all this first started, it was wall-to-wall brooms and buckets. When Adam realized he needed a think tank—boom! He sent all the brooms packing. Sam ran his hand along the desktop. Real mahogany. Adam spent a whole month's budget on that desk. It was far too heavy and far too big for such a small room. Something about it reminded him of his childhood—

"Sam!"

Sam turned to Addy and wrapped his arms round her shoulders.

They clung to each other for nearly three minutes before Sam dared speak.

"Is it the gambler or the alcoholic in me that attracts you most?"

"Stop. I love you despite those things." Addy turned her head to hide her expression. What did I just say?

What did she just say?

"Sam, please don't look at me that way, not now."

Addy nodded sideways, gesturing toward the door.

"I'm going to head out now," Addy called to Wendy.

Sam stood still, afraid to move, afraid to look at Addy.

"Bye, Sam."

Sam didn't respond.

Addy punched him in the arm.

"Why'd you hit me?"

"Sam," Addy whispered, "wait two minutes, then meet me in the parking lot."

Sam dreamt of this moment a thousand times. He could anticipate her every word, her every movement.

As Addy opened her apartment door, Sam doubled over in pain.

"What's wrong?"

"I can't breathe."

"Here, sit down. Do you have asthma?"

"No." Sam coughed. "Anxiety. This is my first time."

"For what?"

"You know … the birds and bees thing."

Addy smiled. "Sam, are you a bird or a bee?"

"I hope I'm not a bird. They scare me. Birds, clowns, spiders, snakes—"

"Got it, not a bird. How about we do the bee and blossom instead?"

"And I'd be…."

"The bee who hadn't stung anyone."

"And you're the bosom?"

"Blossom."

"Sorry, I sometimes mix up words when I'm nervous."

"Relax." Addy ran her hand through Sam's hair.

"Is there something special in your bedroom?"

"You'd prefer the bedroom?"

"It's just—"

She kissed him.

"It's just that I—"

She kissed him again.

"I dreamt about your gun."

"Funny, I dreamt about your gun, too." Addy unbuttoned the top button of her blouse. "One."

"Addy, wait—"

"I can't. Two." Addy unbuttoned the second button.

"I have a gun, a toy gun."

"Shh. Our guns are real. Three."

"Yours was on a stand in your bedroom, on your *katanakake.*"

"Four."

"Adam warned me—"

"He warned you about what?" She refastened the fourth button.

"Nothing about you."

"Nothing? Not even the color of my blossoms?" The lake in her eyes turned to rough sea as she closed the third button.

"No, of course not … he never mentioned anything about mostly white with a tinge of red."

"A tinge of red!"

"I'm teasing! He just told me a man-to-man thing."

"Like what?"

"To take it slow—"

"Slowly," she corrected before resuming her seduction. "Three."

"And not to waste ammo."

"Not to waste ammo?"

"There's an amazing echo in this room."

"Explain yourself," she threatened, reaching back for button three.

"A man has only so many rounds, you know, in his gun, before he starts shooting blanks."

"Nonsense."

"It's a big deal for me."

"Adam's wrong. I can't believe he told you that."

"Well, he didn't say it in so many words—"

"What happened?"

"He drew a lot of depressing pictures and then made me watch some hour-long infomercial."

"Scare tactics. It isn't like you're packing a six-shooter."

"Adam said you'd say that."

"No, he didn't."

"Yes, he did. He said a clever woman can lure a man into having sex by saying things like 'it isn't like you're packing a six-shooter.'"

"Unbelievable!"

"Right … till I double confirmed it. But luckily, there are these little pills, one's purple and one's blue. Either would upgrade my rig."

"Your rig?"

"To a high capacity magazine."

"And you bought that?"

"Of course not! I don't read magazines. Too much gossip and fashion, though in a pinch, I'll scavenge for an old—"

"I can't believe this."

"It's true. You can learn all kinds of stuff. Like in 1965, I think, there was an article about a curse on an island. People went to find treasure but ended up spending their whole lives there just digging and digging."

"Sounds tragic."

"Adam said you'd understand once I explained everything."

Addy's eyes narrowed, turning to pools of black. She buttoned her blouse.

"He kept mumbling on about how you're way out of my league. 'Even if she loved you six times in a row,' he said, 'she'd wake up wishing she hadn't.'"

"You must be kidding."

"No, he actually said 'six times in a row.'"

Addy's face went blank.

"Sorry, he meant you'd wish you hadn't loved me, not that you'd wish you hadn't woken up. I told Adam that wasn't very clear. Woken? Is it 'woken'?"

"Stop."

"But he insisted—"

"Insisted?"

"He said, 'Look at her.'" Sam looked deeply into Addy's eyes. "'She's beautiful.'" Addy softened. "'And smart. Her eyes sparkle like the North Star and there's no one better to help you find your way.'" Sam put his hand on Addy's shoulder. "Will you help me find my way?"

"Let's empty that six-shooter of yours."

"Uh-oh."

"What's wrong now?"

"The first round went off."

She kissed him.

"Oops, that's two."

Sam squirmed as Addy took off her blouse, revealing white blossoms tinged with red.

"That's three. And four."

"Relax, you still have two shots left."

"Should I announce them?"

"No, they'll speak for themselves."

Sam touched Addy's shoulder. She didn't wake. Saturday mornings were meant for sleep.

Sam tapped again. "Roll over, plover."

"I think it's pronounced plover."

Sam swirled his finger on the side of Addy's neck just above where it met her shoulder.

"Your hand's cold." She buried her face in her pillow.

"Addy, if you're not really an atheist and all, I know what I want for Christmas."

Addy looked up, then covered her eyes. Someone had opened the curtain.

"I think atheists are probably good at gift giving … you know, to make up for all that guilt."

Her pillow pulled her back into slumber.

"I think I'd like a tiller."

"Ah-huh."

"Adam had one. It was little but it went deep."

"I know."

"You know?"

"I saw it with my own eyes."

Sam got up and started pacing. "Addy, was last night pity sex? That felt like pity sex."

"How do you know what pity sex feels like?"

"I've dreamt many, many times about having pity sex."

Addy turned over and looked at Sam. "That reminds me. Why did you raise your hand?"

"In my sleep?"

"Yes."

"Like asking a question?"

"Yes."

"No reason. I mean … it probably wasn't me."

"Okay, but after we shower, I'm going to dress up like a school teacher and we'll see who raises their hand."

Sam didn't respond. He didn't hug or kiss her. He didn't even try to get up from his tiny wooden desk. He never had a crush on a teacher. He never raised his hand in class.

"Addy?"

"Sam, be a good bee and go back to sleep."

"Can I at least thank you?"

"For what? Pity sex?"

"For not saying what you're really thinking."

"And what's that?"

"You're asking yourself why you're in this lopsided relationship."

Addy rolled back onto her stomach.

Sam waited nearly two minutes before tapping. "Addy?"

"Stop buzzing."

"Addy, why isn't there an entrance exam for sex?"

Addy sat up. She was beautiful. He felt his gun reloading. He wanted to raise both hands and ask her to marry him. But what if she said no? What if she just laughed?

"Sam, why would you want to risk failing such a test?"

"I was thinking of it as a placement test—you know, to minimize unintentional weapon fire."

"Four volleys before we got your pants off ... that's gotta be some kind of record."

"Don't make fun of my marksmanship. I don't get to the range very often ... and you didn't warn me you were in full bloom."

"Que será, será. Whatever will bee, will bee. Maybe next time you'll only get off three shots before we embrace."

"Or maybe I'll fire all six." Sam blushed.

"Oh, honey, I also know what I want for Christmas."

"Okay, sugar. I'll move in next weekend."

Addy's eyes opened wide. She was fully awake now and might never sleep again.

"Sam, listen to me. You can move in on one condition. We share everything, including the rent ... and no one else touches your pistol."

"That's two conditions."

"Going once, twice—"

"I accept."

"Good. You'll need to ask for a raise. We need to stock up on ammo. Maybe get that additional magazine."

"But I don't have time to read."

After breakfast, Addy crawled back into bed.

Sam jumped on the mattress and cried out: "Revolt!"

"No revolting today."

Sam humphed in French. The emperor had no clothes.

Addy turned the page and continued reading.

"Why do you even read the paper? Isn't that already old news?"

"I'll read whichever fake news I so choose, thank you very much."

As Sam reached into a large bag, his eyes were glued on Addy's long fingers smeared with black ink.

"At least my fake news doesn't get ink all over the sheets."

Addy put the paper down. She didn't ask why he was eating so soon after breakfast. She didn't complain about his chocolate-covered lips. But she did rub two fingers across the morning headline and then across the top sheet.

Sam crawled under the covers, shimmying left and right in exaggerated waves as he paddled lower and lower, down the bed.

When Addy woke, Sam was gone. No note, no call. He missed work altogether.

He returned three days later. He hadn't shaved or showered.

"Clean up. We need to talk."

As the warm water loosened his neck, Sam realized his relationship with Addy might be over. He hadn't been gambling, but she wouldn't believe him.

Sam stepped into the bedroom wearing only a towel. Addy was already in bed.

"Addy?"

"Come to bed, Sam."

"I can't, not yet."

"Why not?"

"I have a confession to make."

Addy sat up and turned on the bedside lamp. She was listening.

"I'm not sure I'm cut out to be a comedian. I've been working my butt off and nothing's clicking."

"Maybe you're trying too hard."

"I have to work harder than the other comedians."

"But you're funny."

"Maybe in the bedroom, but not on stage. The pressure gets to me … it's always crippled me since I was five."

"Sam, tell me what you're feeling."

"When I was young, I knew I was different. I didn't fit in. So I went to the library."

"The library?"

"To get some joke books. I figured tell a joke here, there, maybe make a friend. But after I read all the books—"

"You couldn't tell what was funny?"

"I had the best jokes memorized. I even categorized them by target audience, time of day, and necessary prop."

"By prop? That makes sense, I guess."

"Please stop kidding around. I'm being deadly serious here."

"Okay, so you knew the jokes … so?"

"I had no idea what to do next. Should I fire a series of quick ones, maybe sequence them to setup a cleanup batter?"

"A cleanup batter?"

"Yes, humor's like baseball. You get a couple runners on base, then hit them home with your strongest wood."

"I like the sound of that."

"Addy, please."

"Sorry." She wasn't the least bit sorry. In fact, she was getting angry. No, she was already pissed. He was the one AWOL for most of the week.

"Are you with me, Addy?"

A smile sparked across her face.

Sam lost track of his next point as he watched Addy bite her lip once, twice. He dropped his towel and jumped into bed.

Morning came despite Sam's attempt to stall the inevitable. He hadn't slept. How could she possibly love him?

"Good morning, Sam."

"I want to tell you—"

"Oh, right, do finish your story."

"It's not important."

"Of course it's important. Tell me. I want to hear it."

"Okay. I tried but I couldn't do it."

"Sam—" Addy stopped herself. It was almost a minute before Sam continued.

"I wrote jokes on index cards and ordered them with the funniest on top. Then I had to go to the bathroom…."

"Sam!" Addy caught herself. Better to let him talk or she'll never get breakfast.

"I had to rehearse. Time was running out. So, I'm watching myself in the mirror—"

"And? Sorry."

"And nothing. I told my first joke and not a peep—even I didn't laugh."

"I'm gonna skip breakfast. I need to ... something's waiting for me at the—"

"Okay, but—"

"Gotta run. See you at work!"

She disappeared without shutting the door.

He couldn't help but watch Addy as she called for the elevator once, twice, a dozen times. She mashed that button over and over again.

She wanted out. He could see that now.

Sam tore a sheet from Addy's notebook. He didn't notice the writing on the back of the page.

What could he say that would make any difference? She already knew everything about him. Well, almost everything. She didn't know the truth. Tonight, tomorrow, or the next day, she would wonder why he hadn't returned. But her disappointment wouldn't last. She would turn this last page and close their book.

Twenty minutes passed before Sam wrote a word. When he looked up, his eyes searched for something.

"Adam? It's Sam."

"Sam who?"

"I need to confess something."

"Uh-huh, like the time you set the neighbor's outbuilding on fire?"

"It was concrete block. It wouldn't have burned down."

"So what then?"

"My secret will hurt someone I love, but I have to tell her before I leave."

"Hurt like a bee sting or—"

"I pee in the shower!"

Sam lied. Yes, he peed in the shower, but that wasn't his secret.

"Cross that out!"

"Okay, let me run some water and then we'll see how you feel."

Sam crossed it out three times but he could still see the pee.

"Stop. What's really bothering you?"

"She's too much for me."

"I know what you mean."

"You said that was an accident."

"Nothing happened between us."

"Are your fingers crossed?"

"Not anymore. Just tell her you love her."

"Of course I love her. Everybody loves her."

"Beauty is a curse."

Sam wrote: "I love you. Beauty is a curve."

"Curse, not curve. Cross it out."

"Isn't it sort of both?"

"You don't know what you're doing, do you?"

"How could I?" Sam scratched on the paper. "I'm not allowed to pee or love."

"She just needs her space."

"Yeah, I get that."

"You shouldn't have moved in. It was too soon."

"I snore!"

"You're not worthy because you snore?"

"Oh, right." He crossed it out. "I did sabotage the sonic cannon. Should I write that?"

"Just ask her to forgive you. And don't forget to write her once you get wherever you're going."

He grabbed his coat and took one last look. He struggled to pull her key from his pocket, almost crushing the note before placing it gently on the table by the front door.

"We just weren't right for each other," he repeated over and over again till he flagged a taxi.

"We need to stop at my place, then on to the airport … there's a fiver in it for you if we get there by two."

The driver started to laugh but stopped when he saw Sam's expression in the rear view mirror. The cheap bastard wasn't joking.

Raikiri

SAM looked for the shortest line.

"Can I help you, sir?"

"Yes, thank you."

"Are you a Double Blue Diamond Solitaire Platinum member?"

"I think I have your Carbide card—"

"That won't do, sir. This is the Double Blue Diamond—"

"Solitaire Platinum line, I know, but—"

"Sorry, sir, but we don't allow buts." The ticket clerk smiled as she shrugged her shoulders. "Rules are rules."

"I understand; it's just that my alarm didn't ring and if I don't get on this flight...." He waled. "I'll miss my wedding."

He had her full attention. "What flight, sir?"

"First class, Tokyo."

"Flight to Tokyo leaves in one hour from gate seventeen. Just need your passport and credit card."

"What's that flight go for?"

"Twelve hours to Tokyo, fourteen on the way back."

"I meant how much does it cost?"

"First class, twenty thousand and—"

Sam didn't hear how many hundreds of dollars. His ears had turned off.

"How much for coach?"

"Sir, this is the Double Blue—"

"I know. How much for one-way coach?"

"The gentleman over there can point you to the bus depot."

"How much to swim?"

An older couple laughed. They were in the non-Double-Blue-Diamond line with a herd of other travelers.

Sam shook his head. Maybe humans were cattle.

"Young man?" Sam turned to find the scruffy voice.

"Have we met?"

"I don't think so." The elderly man answered as he introduced his wife. Sam didn't hear her name. He was too busy thinking about what he would say next.

"Thanks for laughing at my joke."

"We both like to swim." The man paused, turning to his wife. "Yes, dear, I told him we don't travel much anymore."

"Not since that HD."

"She means not since our television started working again. I hadn't seen a football game for nearly forty years."

"He eats in front of that thing."

"Now, we don't need to bother this young man with all our aches and pains." He cupped his hand round his mouth. "This one has the biggest pain of all."

"I heard you."

"If you heard me, what did I say?"

She slapped his shoulder. "You know it's my back. It knots up like the dickens."

He tried to kiss her but she pushed him away.

"Sorry, I have to get going."

"To Japan?" she asked. "Are you sure?"

"You know he has to meet his wife."

"She ain't his wife yet. And she could be in Chicago for all I know."

"Don't tie yourself in a knot. We have to take this man at his word."

She whispered something to her husband.

"No, he's not the one."

"Ask him."

"She thinks we saw you at the nine o'clock."

"The seven-thirty. You ain't been up past nine since Dwight. God rest his soul."

"I'm just starting. It wasn't me."

The old man pulled Sam aside. "Have you thought about a desk job?"

"Leave that poor boy alone." She went for her husband's shoulder but missed. "He's got the funny gene."

"Now why'd you go and box my ear?"

"It's not that bad. You're hardly bleeding. Should we call the 911?" She turned to Sam. "You know, when we were younger, we traveled to Japan on a boat. It's all we could afford."

"It was a ship. We went through Singapore."

"I'm sorry, but I really have to get going."

"Too busy for us, now that you're a big shot?"

"I'm nobody."

"Everybody's somebody. God made sure of that."

The trip would be long and arduous. Sam wasn't sure if the ship would drop anchor in Osaka or in some other Japanese port. He never asked. All that mattered was finding his sea legs.

On the third day he woke to a grumbling tummy. Meals were included, right? He'd act like he belonged when he joined the chow line.

Sam reached for the pepper but found none. He swallowed the powdered eggs in bits and pieces. A single egg might last the whole journey.

He felt alone. He accidentally swallowed another bite. He reached for his cup, careful to prevent other morsels from sliding down his throat.

Was this water safe to drink? Or was it laced with invisible crawly things? Sam raised his cup to get a better look.

A cheer sprang from the shabby crowd. Several men took long drags from their mugs. Sam smiled as those men laughed and laughed. Their happiness was contagious.

Sam looked around the cabin. Many glasses were raised in anticipation. Perhaps Sam wasn't the only one eating a first meal at sea. So many eyes were waiting, waiting and watching, still watching.

Sam put the cup to his lips and swallowed. If he died tonight, this swill would have an accomplice. Peer pressure gets ugly so fast.

"Thank you, sir," an elderly man said as he sat down near Sam. "We weren't sure if it was safe to drink."

"You speak English?"

"English is native to Singapore. My wife and I thank you. We have been so very ill and so very thirsty. We knew the ale was safe, but the water?"

"I wish you both the best. We now share the same fate."

Sam nodded as he excused himself to return to his bunk. He was glad to discover his belongings were still beside the bed. As he unpacked his bag, he discovered a folder.

"So, that's where *Raikiri*'s been hiding."

The words "Top Secret" were in red on the front cover. He didn't recall those words being written in red. He looked up. The whole room seemed cast in red, everything was some shade of red or gray. The *Raikiri* pages were pink, his skin black—

"Damn it!"

The pen wouldn't write. He tried a second pen. These test scribbles were red. Surprise, surprise. Maybe the water had damaged his eyes.

He searched the folder for the copy of the painting. He remembered the image if only because it seemed a strange addition to this file, any file really. It was out of place; it wasn't even good art. Why would Adam include it? Why would he want to remind himself of his struggle to paint barely interesting features? Wouldn't a more extreme angle have been a better choice?

Maybe all the lines and rectangles were meant to convey more than the historical image. He hoped so. He was on his way to that very city. This painting had to be a clue, not just an exercise in perspective. Could fate be that cruel?

Love certainly was.

Sam panicked. He shuffled through the pages again. It wasn't there.

He shook the folder. A page fell free, landing on the floor. It was the print. It looked mysterious. A treasure map? No, no X on either side. And wouldn't an X typically be in red?

Not possible this time. The copy was black and white. But why? Wouldn't that make searching for clues more difficult?

Sam extended both railings until they intersected. "There's an *X*."

"Unless it's upside down."

"*X*s can't be upside down."

Sam turned the print ninety degrees. Nothing. He turned it again. The negative space of the sky couldn't be a clue, could it? What shape did it make? Sam outlined the edge of the sky with his pen. The amorphous shape could be anything, a plot of land, a skyline, even a landmark.

The clock struck 5:00. Addy left work without saying goodbye.

It was raining. She paused at the top of the stairs. She had forgotten her umbrella but luckily had remembered to put the top up.

Once inside her car, she couldn't stop thinking about Sam. What happened? Where was he? How could she share her life with someone who doesn't show up? She leaned her head against the steering wheel.

Dinner? Stop for a drink?

Maybe Sam had fallen and hit his head. Amnesia?

She didn't recall anything after starting the car. Before she realized it, she was running up the third flight of stairs. She stared at the numbers nailed to her door before wrapping her hand round the knob. She wasn't ready for what she might find.

She dropped her keys on the entry table as she ran to the bedroom. No sign of him on or under the bed. On to the bathroom … no blood in the shower.

"This isn't funny. When I find him, I'm gonna break his nose."

She stumbled back into the living room and kicked the front door shut.

"What's that?"

A folded sheet caught her eye. She grabbed for the note, pulling it to her chest. This note would explain everything.

"To Addy." So far, so good. She hesitated. Sam hadn't been careful as he wrote her name, as he folded the paper. Nor had he torn the page from the notebook with much care. Squirrelly bits marred the edge of this love note. Or was it something worse?

It read: "I sabotaged the sonic cannon. Forgive me."

It made no sense. He couldn't have tampered with the hardware or programming. He was in Osaka.

Why was phrase after phrase crossed out, repeated and crossed out again? Was he arguing with himself? Couldn't he find another sheet of paper and try again? She turned the note over.

"He ripped this page from my journal!"

Addy pulled into the driveway. She hadn't been here since her mother died. She didn't go in. She started to walk. It didn't matter where; she needed to clear her head.

"Addy?"

"Ben!"

"It's so great to see you!"

She didn't respond; she was busy admiring his—

"What brings you to town?"

"Just visiting. I never sold the family home. What have you been up to?"

"We're converting Harley's into a dinner theater. See?" Ben pointed to the marquee. "Come on in."

"It's beautiful."

"We've salvaged as much of the original wood as we could."

"Who's that?"

"My partner. Hey, Mel, come here!"

"Excuse the dust."

"Mel, this is Addy. Addy, Mel."

"Nice to meet you."

"You've done a wonderful job. Are those wall hangings from the original bar?"

"Some sections of the bar top had such great carvings. That one is my favorite."

Addy squinted; she couldn't quite make out who loved whom.

"How long have you known Ben?"

"Like forever."

Ben laughed. "She's my little sister."

Addy smiled uncontrollably.

"I think she likes you."

Addy blushed. She was afraid to look at Ben.

"Addy, I have an idea: why don't you join us for opening night next month?"

"Or the month after that … we haven't finished casting yet." Little sister glared at big brother. "He has thousands of friends in NYC, but somehow none of them are right."

"It's my first play. It has to be perfect."

"First play for your new theater or did you write it?"

"Yes, both." Ben's tired eyes sparkled. "Finding the right lead will put this place on the map."

"He calls it Off-Off-Off-Broadway."

Ben looked in the coat closet. "Mel, where are the scripts?"

"In a box somewhere. We're supposed to finish sanding today, remember?"

"I'll have to send you one."

"Are you about to ask for her number, big brother?"

Sam had no clue where to find *Raikiri*, but he could learn more about the infamous blade while looking for hints in Adam's research. Where to begin? Maybe the first question to ask about any legendary object is: was it real? People have bizarre imaginations. Anything can be a hoax. His grandmother never believed we landed on the moon.

What do we know? Swords exist. Same for samurais. Do such warriors still serve? Unclear but likely irrelevant when studying a sixteenth century legend.

But can a sword cut lightning?

Maybe the sword's name was an exaggeration, a hint of truth that grew to myth over the years. Maybe the fear wrought by *Raikiri* cut down enemies before the blade itself had the chance.

A chill went down Sam's spine.

Back to the facts.

A master swordsmith forged a unique weapon. The sword found its way to Tachibana Dōsetsu who did his samurai thing for like sixty years. He died in battle at seventy-two.

"Note to self: if I ever find *Raikiri*, remind me to stop attacking castles before turning seventy-two."

What happened to such a sword when a samurai passed on? A child or other family member would likely inherit the legacy. But what if that new owner didn't want to be a samurai? What if an entire family line sought the promises of higher education and refused the weapon?

Sam laughed. "The pen would be mightier than the sword."

His eyes opened wide. Would they have to hide it? It was valuable and dangerous. They wouldn't want an evil emperor or outcast villain to possess its power. They would lock it away where no one would stumble upon it. They would have to entrust the protection of the sword to a line of strong but unambitious warriors who wouldn't steal the sword for their own glory.

But what if many generations later an exception was born, someone who was more than scholar? What if this warrior woman wanted the sword? What if she had red hair and lived near a secret time travel laboratory in Pennsylvania?

Wouldn't Addy want *Raikiri*? Wouldn't she deserve her family's legacy?

Sam remembered the empty *katanakake* on Addy's bedroom wall.

He would find her this sword. He would find *Raikiri*.

Addy spent her morning tightening screws. She planned to move on to nuts in the afternoon. Someone or something would pay for her pain.

"Addy?" Addy ignored Wendy. "Addy, let's have lunch."

Addy wiped her forehead and reached for an even bigger screwdriver.

"Addy, stop. You're beautiful, inside and out."

"What difference does that make?" She searched the toolbox, but couldn't find the right wrench. She was so ready for those nuts.

"You could be with anyone."

"Don't try to console me. I'm already over him."

"Good for you." Wendy watched Addy's eyes still filled with anger. "So, Addy, what do you really want?"

"I don't want things. I want what any woman, what any person needs."

"S'mores?"

Addy laughed. "No, silly. Fulfillment."

"Looking for this?"

"Yes, pass me that wretch. I need to torque something."

Sam knew where to start his search for *Raikiri*. He counted the subway stops on the station map and boarded the train. The car was mostly full. He steadied himself as the doors began to close.

A woman raced toward the train. Her long black hair flowed behind. Her white blouse inched up from the waist of her skirt—midriff bare, fit, mid-twenties. But the scarf? She would not have chosen that scarf.

Her hand pounded on the cold barrier. The urgency fell from her face as the car lurched forward, pulling away. Sam imagined her running beside the train, her lips pressed against the glass. So much in life was here one moment and gone the next.

The tension broke as the train slowed for the next station. Sam watched for a message board, something which shared the schedule of incoming trains. Two minutes.

This train was less crowded. Sam sat near the door. In two stops, he would reach his destination and start scouting for clues. He checked his pockets for his map and sketches.

How many years would that woman sacrifice, mourning missed trains … living with a man who didn't love her? Maybe if she had worn red, things would have turned out differently.

Once outside the train, Sam looked for an emergency device on the closing door. He laughed as he spotted a big red button. It had to be a big red button. Such buttons would soon take over the world. In a few years we would sleep, eat, even have sex at the push of a button. Sam closed his eyes. He wished he hadn't put sex buttons on the table.

A sign stretched across the street announcing Sam's arrival at Dōtonbori. Bright colors, oversized signs, and papier-mâché sculptures jumped from the buildings, forcing thousands of spectators through a funnel of carnival delights. Sam walked for thirty minutes before stopping to catch his breath. His stomach growled but dinner would have to wait. There was only an hour of daylight left and he needed to show his sketches to as many people as possible.

Sam looked up at a large lobster clawing the side of a building. It wasn't the Godzilla-like creature that caught his attention. He had seen that lobster before—or a very similar one. Was he going in circles? Was this place really as immense as it seemed? Had all the state fairs been strung together, all the cows and chickens and pigs been replaced with squid, lobster and chubby faces?

Sam maneuvered through the crowd to position himself in front of a convenience store. He stood close to a crossroads and yet sheltered from herds of pedestrians. He opened his map and readied his sketches.

"Can we help you?" a couple offered.

"Yes, thank you. I'm lost. I'm looking for a building that looks like this."

"Sorry, maybe you should try Tokyo."

Sam turned to face the Mardi Gras parade flowing from the opposite direction. He wished he had beads to pass out to all the beaming women.

"May we help you?" an older couple without any beads asked.

"Yes, thank you. I'm lost. I'm trying to find a mountain that looks like this."

"Mount Fuji?" the wife offered.

"Maybe Ishizuchi?" the husband countered.

"Too far! This island, please!" She touched her spouse on the shoulder in hopes of preventing such a mistake in the future.

"Nantai-san, then," he suggested, watching for her reaction.

"Hai. Nantai-san." It was their first agreement in forty years.

"Thank you!" Sam bowed. The couple returned the bow. Sam bowed lower. The wife tried to bow even lower but couldn't. "Gomen'nasai," Sam whispered.

The wife smiled as she raised her hand to her ear.

"Gomen'nasai," Sam repeated loudly.

Every man should learn the native word for sorry.

"Where's Nantai-san?"

"Near Tokyo," the man answered, pointing to the east.

"Look to the north," the woman suggested.

"Tokyo is east of Osaka."

"Yes, dear, but Nantai-san is north of Tokyo."

"Of course, the volcano is north of Tokyo."

The wife's expression changed. "The sacred mountain has not erupted for ten thousand years, but no one can predict such things."

Addy smiled when she found a broken wire in stage three.

"Adam must have had a bad day."

She blinked and all her heroes were gone.

She fixed the issue without a second thought and latched the chassis door. This too would soon be a distant memory.

Jiggety-jig

THE sound of falling water drew Sam closer to the shrine at the foot of Mount Nantai. A twisted rope spanned the temple's entrance. Four lightning-shaped streamers adorned the simple rope. Sam made an offering to bless his climb before starting up the wide stone steps. The path led to a steeper staircase with a metal railing up the center.

The ground soon turned rough, hewed by the axe of an ancient mountain god. Rows of stick trees seemed as unshaven hairs. But no blade could best the roots and rocks, stumps and shards which rose from the skin of this great volcano. No step was sure. And yet, in any second, an outstretched arm could touch the sky.

As the trail turned to pavement, Sam stopped to drink from his bottle. The water tasted sweet. Only forty-five minutes into a four-hour climb and he was ready to sing praises to filtered water. Sam bowed to the water before washing the sweat from his brow.

A few hikers were sprinkled on the edge of the road. A few more on a grass mound cresting along side a small building. Sam scanned the faces of the mostly young travelers. Had he hoped to recognize someone? He noticed the marker for Station Four. He hadn't seen the other stones. An auspicious entrance framed a set of concrete steps which shrank as they twisted up and out of sight. He wasn't ready for all the unknowns that hid beyond that bend. He yearned for a bed but would gladly settle for a bench.

He turned to face the lookout. The small square shelter rested on another square, an odd cement block foundation open on one end. An old man sat on a large nearby rock.

"Sir?" No response. "Sir-san?"

The man laughed without acknowledging Sam.

"I don't have much to offer, sir, but I'd gladly give you all I have to sit on your rock."

The man slid to his left and tapped twice on the now open seat.

"Thank you."

"Your shoes."

"My shoes?"

"You offered me anything. I accept your shoes as a gift for the mountain god."

Sam began to unlace his left shoe.

The old man laughed uncontrollably, looking at Sam for the first time. "You are quite suppliant and yet I am not a god."

Sam tied his shoe.

"Do you not honor your word?"

"I haven't lived long enough to know my worth."

"I accept your honesty as payment for all debts." As he studied Sam, the old man's face grew more and more inquisitive. "Pardon my curiosity, but is it true you own nothing?"

Sam nodded.

"And you know nothing?"

Sam nodded.

"Such a man with nothing must want of something."

"Somedays, a cup of water and a bowl of rice is enough." Sam chuckled. "And, of course, a place to sit."

"Yes, for a body this is good. But for a soul? Does your soul not toil for something?"

"You wouldn't believe me if I told you."

"I am an old man. I have heard many things."

"Yes, I'm sure you have." Sam hesitated. Something about this man was oddly familiar. "Is it true there's a blade at the summit? One which pierces through rock and points to heaven?"

"It is one of many, not the sword you seek."

"I never said anything about a specific sword."

"My apologies, Sam-san. You are a man in search of his destiny, so when you asked about the sword at the summit...." The man smiled. "Perhaps you have come so far across the world for exercise? Or to fix my television?"

Sam got up. His face turned apologetic. "Sorry, I'm not from Samsung. I don't know how to fix TVs or anything really."

"If you are not Sam-san or from Samsung, then who are you?"

"I'm just a traveler who must be going. Stage five awaits and I really want to see the volcanic rock near the summit."

"If you have seen Mars, you already know such rock—"

"What?"

"If you venture farther up this mountain, I will not be here when you return."

Sam nodded. "Then I'll say goodbye. We'll each walk our own path."

"Walking a path is more errand than quest. Only a reluctant hero holds to a path. So, tell me, why are you here?"

"Promise you won't laugh."

"I never laugh."

"You've laughed at me twice already."

"I never laugh at samurai."

"I'm looking for *Raikiri*."

"*Raikiri*? A true quest."

"You know of—"

"Every soul on this island knows of *Raikiri*. Why would you want such a thing?"

"I've been swarmed by a thousand birds and struck by lightning—"

"You know both *Chidori* and *Raikiri*?"

"Somedays, I know everything … and the next, nothing."

"Then you should go quickly before you forget again."

"I should go? Are you dismissing me or giving me a clue?"

"A little of both. I yearn for a hot bath. Is that a letter in your pocket? May I mail it for you?"

"Yes, thank you. I should have mailed it twenty years ago."

"This I can do."

Sam started up the hill to stage five.

"Not that path." The man pointed. "Go that way until you reach a modest mountain, travel halfway to the summit and rest on the bench near the brook."

"I didn't catch that last word? Did you say 'book'?"

The man's face grew weary.

"I'm not trying to be an ass."

"I understand, Sam-san. It comes naturally for you."

"It's just that I keep imagining myself halfway up a strange mountain, looking for the wrong clue. I can't have come this far to fail because I misheard a single word."

"Brook … rest on the bench near the brook." The man waved goodbye with the letter in his hand. "There is a beautiful view where all things are possible."

Sam smiled. "Brook" made way more sense. He scanned the horizon but couldn't see a thing. The hilltop hid behind a thick mist. Sam turned to say thank you, but the old man had already gone.

Sam laughed. The modest mountain was more hill than mountain. Halfway up, he could hear the sound of water behind a grove of red pines. He followed his ears through the trees and down a grassy bank to the edge of the brook. A path of stones led across the water.

No bench in sight. He studied the brook. One or more of those stones might fall away if stepped on. He knelt in the mud for guidance.

He heard a giggle in the distance but saw no one.

He tried the first stone with only a portion of his weight. It was solid as was the next. Sam lingered on the second stone. Was the third one a trap? It was by far the smallest and most likely to be a weak link. Erosion could have carved out the sediment under that far corner—

Another giggle.

"Not helpful." Sam jumped over the third stone and landed nearly squarely on the fourth. His foot got a little wet.

Once on the far side of the brook, Sam listened for the next giggle. Nothing. He raced up the hill, scanning the tree line. Was that it? He was winded by the time he reached the forest. There were thousands of nearby stones, but only one on wooden legs. It was quite comfortable.

"May I join you?" a familiar voice asked.

Sam leaped to his feet. "Yes, please."

She bowed ever so slightly before sitting on the far left of the great stone.

"The bench is quite sturdy."

She giggled. "Please sit."

"May I?"

She nodded but Sam did not sit. "A couple in Dōtonbori told me about Mount Nantai. An old man on Nantai-san showed me the way to this bench."

"And?" she asked.

"He said the view would be beautiful."

"A wise man. Do you agree?"

"Yes, the view is magnificent."

"I am Luscious—"

Sam tried not to giggle.

"I am Luscious," she repeated, "guardian queen of this mountain."

"You are a goddess?"

"What do you think?"

"You look like a goddess."

She smiled. "Your eyes do not deceive you, Sam."

"You know me? How?"

"This is not our first time."

"Wow, I do feel a little déjà vu."

"What if I told you we made love the last time we met?"

"I guess I'd start by saying thank you."

Luscious smiled.

"But if we were together, it must have been before I met Addy."

"Is Addy so beautiful?"

"She stirs every limb of every tree. Her breath is the wind."

Sam's cleverness pleased her. "On such a lonely mountain, any woman can carry a thousand plovers with a single word."

"Let me write that down. You are the keeper of all treasures."

"You think me a dragon?"

Sam hesitated. "Only if you wish to be a dragon."

"So we agree. Show me one more kindness and I will grant your deepest desire."

"Though I am no samurai, I seek *Raikiri*."

Her eyes grew maleficent. "The old man does not speak to those in search of treasure. Be gone."

"Forgive me. I meant no disrespect. The treasure I seek is not the sword."

"I am a dragon who cares not for riddles. You have but one last chance before I—"

"You are beautiful, a true goddess who rules this mountain and the hearts of every plover … but not my heart; my soul belongs to another."

"Love is not a stone which only one hand may hold. Love is the wind. You cannot deny the wind its kiss."

"But I do."

"You should go."

Sam turned to head back. He watched his feet to avoid tripping on endless roots, countless stones. He was on his way home. He needed to get there in one piece.

As he reached the foothills, an object called to Sam. He ran toward the shimmering light. He balanced his prize in both hands. He tugged at the hilt, but *Raikiri*'s blade would not yield.

Sam woke as the sun peeked over the horizon. He tore strips from his shirt to fashion a makeshift rope which he wrapped over his shoulder and around his waist. A few more knots would secure the sword.

The walk to the harbor seemed a lifetime. He missed her with every step.

At last, he could see the sun dancing on water. As he readied to board the vessel, he cradled his treasure in unworthy hands. *Raikiri* deserved a samurai.

"Thank you. I would have never made it this far without you."

A sudden vibration startled him. He pulled on the hilt and scabbard, revealing the sword's mirrored surface. He spread his arms to draw the sword. Electricity jumped from the blade to his fingertips and back again. The nearly invisible edge whispered back and forth as it sliced through air.

Sam paused to decipher the weapon's inscription: 雷切. He laughed. "It probably said something like, 'We search for what we already hold.'"

"All aboard!" rang out from a loudspeaker as a middle-aged Japanese man approached Sam.

"I am sorry to inform you, sir. All weapons must be checked before boarding."

"I relinquish my sword." Sam presented the sword to the steward.

"Thank you, Driver-*dono*." The steward studied the etching. "It is a beautiful blade." He lifted the weapon and pointed. "These characters speak to the name. The first symbol means 'lightning' and the second one 'cut.'"

"That can't be!"

"Sorry, the two symbols when combined say *Raikiri* or Lightning Cutter."

"*Raikiri*, right!" Both men smiled. The steward motioned for Sam to climb aboard.

"All aboard!" clanged across the peer.

"All aboard, sir."

There was no time, but he had to know. "The inscription says nothing about birds, nothing about lots of birds?"

"No, it says only…." He turned the sword over. "Oh, here, a second inscription." He pointed to 千鳥. "This is *Chidori* which means 'A Thousand Birds.'"

The steward bowed as he presented *Raikiri* to its master.

Sam returned a bow as he accepted his sword. "So, one side says *Raikiri* and the other says *Chidori*?"

"*Hai*, Driver-*dono*. One is the old name and one the new. It was once a plover in a flock of snipes … till it cut the Thunder God from within the lightning."

"I don't understand."

"All aboard, final call!" blasted from the speaker as the steward motioned again for Sam to board.

Sam smiled. "A great samurai once wielded this blade."

"As it once was, it shall be again. Final warning, check all weapons before boarding."

Sam presented *Raikiri* and climbed aboard.

"This is a magnificent ship."

"Welcome aboard. She is *The Addison*. Your room is down the corridor on the right."

Sam ran his fingers along Addy's rail. She was both the means and the destination.

The captain shouted all sorts of nonsense as the crew readied the ship. Maybe Sam didn't want to be a captain after all. He tried to laugh, but his heart was heavy. An immense blue stretched out before him.

"I was wrong to want my life to be about me."

A gorgeous violet sunset sparked across the horizon. It was Addy. Her love would bring him home.

CAST PARTY

THE final call sheet requested all cast members appear at four p.m. Addy was first on the scene. She marveled how small the lab seemed from the outside. Had she really spent a whole year inside those walls? A sparse mesh of two-by-fours barely held the set upright. She shivered. One fewer nail and this world would have crumbled months ago.

Sam entered a minute later. He raised a bottle of champagne as their eyes met. He wanted to congratulate her on finally accepting the inheritance, but neither said a word.

Adam and Wendy arrived next. Wendy walked ahead of Adam. It hurt her legs to dawdle. She waved at Sam and Addy with her free hand as she passed them on her way to the break room. She pulled a white cloth from her bag and spread it across the table. There were only two chairs. Had they never had a meal together?

Sam pretended a smile as he filled four glasses. Each actor looked at the others. Without the context of a script, they stood on sacred ground as strangers.

"Speech!" Wendy begged to break the silence.

Sam's face went blank. What was Addy holding?

Say something, anything, Addy pleaded silently.

"I see you got my letter."

"So you did send it."

Sam nodded. "When I was in Japan, looking for *Raikiri.*"

"You couldn't have. I received this letter twenty years ago."

Sam spilled his drink on Addy's blouse. She blocked his hand as he reached for a napkin, then downed her bubbly.

"You wouldn't believe how weird it is to live inside someone's head," Adam said to no one in particular as he headed toward his office. He sat his empty glass on the side table and opened the project log book. An interesting entry caught his eye, something about a SIN app.

"You're a programmer?" Adam called out from his desk.

"Might be a few bugs to work out," Addy shouted back. She was pleased by the compliment and even more relieved Adam wasn't drooling on her shoulder.

"Congratulations," Wendy offered, but Addy heard nothing, standing motionless, drowning in a sea of imaginings. Addy loved and hated Sam more than anyone could realize. In that way, she would always be part of the family.

"Yes, congratulations," Adam agreed, returning to the group. "Both on the production and the programming."

"More champagne, Wen?"

Wendy's glass, still full, sat abandoned on the break table. She didn't drink in novellas or in real life.

Adam sighed and turned away.

"Adam. Thank you for being a good teacher."

A smile rushed over Adam's face.

"I think she meant sensei. Take my word for it, she looks great in black."

Wendy looked extremely uncomfortable.

"Anyway," Sam continued, "of course Addy figured out how to write a phone app. After all, she graduated with an English degree— and everyone knows how hard it is to spell stuff."

"I'll drink to that." Adam remembered the hell that was second-grade spelling.

"Who would have thought an English major would have made me the man I am today?"

Laughter erupted. Addy and Wendy shouted "boy" at the same time.

Sam pushed on. A comedian never waits for laughter to die. "We should toast." Sam cleared his throat as he raised his glass. "To feeling sixteen again—"

"Technically, you were never sixteen."

Wendy squeezed Adam's arm. His face went pale. Even now, his world was defined by her fingertips. He should tell her. Yes, he should tell her.

"Hi, Wen," Adam mumbled.

Something was lost in the translation. Wendy had already moved on. She was drinking heavily from a tumbler of ginger ale as she watched Addy wave one finger.

"One word," Wendy called to Addy.

Addy nodded, then waved two fingers.

"Two syllables."

Addy twisted her hips as she raised her arms.

Sam was ready to play. "Something you take off." Addy shook her head. "Something you put on?"

Addy grew excited, nodding yes, yes. She cupped her hand.

"Starts with *C*."

Addy smiled as she laid down.

"Ends with sleep!" Adam shouted.

Addy glared.

Sam countered, "Ends with dead people?"

Another glare. Addy pointed to her ear, then rubbed her belly.

"Sounds like belly?" both men cried out.

"Sounds like womb," Wendy corrected.

"Tomb!"

"See, it was dead people!"

Addy ran her hands down the sides of her body. Both men became wide-eyed zombies. Wendy knew the answer but refused to continue.

Adam was the first of the dead to wake. "Room, flume, plume...."

"Costume!" Addy agonized. He always took forever to finish.

"Why do you need a costume? Halloween?"

"No, Sam, I've been asked to read for a part."

"For what?"

"*She Could Melt the Sun*. Ben called to squeeze me in. He said I'd be perfect."

"Ben who?"

"He's the director at a playhouse where I grew up."

"Oh! Oh!" Adam interrupted. "Wen, let Addy borrow your witch costume."

"It won't fit. It was for a kindergarten play."

"She was scary good with just a black hat and a huge green nose."

"Are you saying I'd look better with a bigger nose?"

"Never mind him. He's had too much to drink. I'd love to help."

"Thank you, Wendy. I'm thinking something simple in black leather. Tight, but not too tight."

Sam gulped.

"And I'll need something to hold a sword between my shoulders."

A loud alarm shattered the moment. Sam started to fiddle with his watch. Addy punched his arm. Sam ignored her. She would count to four and take him out.

"One."

He mumbled something about getting the right year this time.

"Two."

He pried the back off the watch and flipped one, two—

"Three."

… switches. He strapped the watch on his right wrist.

"You're left handed?"

He spun the knobs on his watch to sixteen, six—

"Four."

Sam's body started to glow. He smiled uncontrollably.

"Sam, where are you going?"

"I need a second chance."

Shhhhikt!

CODA

SAM stopped just before the nurses' station to peer round the corner.

"Uh-oh." He leaned back against the wall, slowly raising his clenched fist to his mouth. "Two suspects, repeat, two suspects. 10-100. Over."

He felt queasy. He checked his pockets. Something important was missing. But what? Something besides a real walkie talkie....

"A cap gun."

A cap gun? Sam laughed. Yes, after all these years, he was a secret agent again. He puffed out his chest, pointed his finger, his Walther PPK. He was ready.

"Doctor."

"Doctor."

Sam kept his eyes forward, his cupped hand smothering his stethoscope as he marched down the hall. He had no time for idolatry.

The nurses watched him till he was out of sight.

"Ass."

"Ass."

Sam's eyes darted from room tag to room tag as he hurried down the maternity floor.

"Ah!" There it was! He had finally found a way back. He took a deep breath as he opened the door.

"Doctor, what's going on? Why can't we see our babies?"

Sam looked into Betty's eyes, then down at his feet. Her eyes, his feet.

"There's a problem."

A crushing silence filled the room. Paul sat down and reached for his wife's hand.

"The bald baby—"

"Adam, the bald one is Adam."

"Adam, right. Adam has a bad heart."

Betty gasped.

"Sorry to be so direct, but we can save only one of them."

Paul looked at Betty, then at the floor. He would be the first to cry.

"I know you have such a difficult decision … but the other baby—"

"Samuel."

"Yes, Samuel." Sam paused. Paul and Betty weren't listening. It was all they could do to hold hands. Their knuckles were white from the force of their bond.

Sam snapped his fingers and immediately regretted his insensitivity. How could he? It was the first time he had seen his parents through his own eyes.

"Baby Samuel has many issues. He's really struggling." Sam too was struggling. "But his heart is strong. We can't save both babies. Will you consent to our giving Sam's heart to Adam?"

Adam too heard Betty's reluctant response. He had lived this moment a thousand times.

Anything is possible.

A Hilltop Book

Lightning Source UK Ltd.
Milton Keynes UK
UKHW010014270721
387818UK00007B/468/J